Justin's GAMBLE

CAROL BRASWELL

Copyright Information

Dedication

To a dear friend, Staci Hayes who outlined Justin's Gamble that set the story in motion. You are priceless.

Acknowledgements

I have to thank my wonderful editor, Alicia Dean. She has been so patient and helpful, I can never thank her enough. My beautiful model, Amy; Elizabeth Martin Photography; Lone Star Harley-Davidson of Tyler, Texas for the loan of the beautiful motorcycle.

Raves for Justin's Gamble

"I just finished reading your book and enjoyed it immensely! This might be my favorite of yours so far. I thought the characters, both minor and major, were well developed, especially Mara, and Justin. The plot was intense, good suspense, and everything flowed really nicely. You were pretty mean to your characters, they never caught a break, LOL, but that's the way it's supposed to be." (Cheril Vernon, Author)

"I loved it. There is action on every page". (Alicia Dean, Author/Editor)

"This is the best you've written." Staci Hayes Wallace

Chapter 1

Justin Garrett clicked the ice in his fourth Jack Daniels of the night. The boring, potbellied veterinarian from Oshkosh, Wisconsin sitting in the next chair kept trying to convince him the best money to be made was in equine dentistry.

The veterinary attendees had gathered early in the Marquee ballroom of the MGM Grand for awards, dinner, and a performance by the Blue Man Group. The entertainment had finished their show an hour ago and he was so ready to get away from the detestable vet who had been glued to his side for two hours.

"I tell you, Garrett, the mouth is the last place a vet pays any attention to." Doctor Wisemiller hushed as a busty waitress in shorts and a skimpy top approached with a tray of drinks. "Well, hello there, cutie." He flashed his yellow crooked teeth. "You wanna come to my pen and play hide-the-weenie?"

The young girl's face turned ten shades of red. She pivoted to walk away. Before she could make her retreat, he grabbed her butt and squeezed. The tray teetered on one hand, and she had no choice but to use her other hand to balance it or lose the drinks.

The obnoxious doctor leered at the young woman. "I can poke you all night and make you very happy." Justin waved his hand letting her know he didn't want any more. Wisemiller sighed when she stepped out of his reach. "I could poke that all night." The doctor smirked.

Justin stared after the attractive girl. She couldn't be a day over twenty-one, with the longest legs he had ever seen. She had the grace of a showgirl the way she moved effortlessly through the crowd. "These women are trying to do a job. Show a little respect and let them work." He stood and set his empty glass on a tray.

"Where you going?" Doctor Wisemiller worked every joint he had to rise from the pale blue couch. The Grand had decorated the Marquee Ballroom in blue to honor the Blue

Man Group. He grabbed his crotch with one hand and shook. "They're all after the same thing. A good lay."

Justin sighed in disgust. This convention had turned out to be a bust. The entertainment had been awesome. It was the best part of the convention so far. Four more days to put up with drunks. He had heard it all in the boozy conversations, from how their wives had wanted to come to which one of the waitresses was willing to go back to their room. A few of the doctors had already ventured into the MGM bars to find hookers or to get smashed before going to bed.

The fake smoke from the show still hung in the air like a cloud. The smell along with a variety of over used colognes hovered like a blanket that was about to suffocate him. He needed fresh air and it was a long walk to the exit. He waited until Wisemiller was engaging another waitress in a whispered conversation before starting for the lobby.

He spotted the exit sign and wove through the maze of tables and other veterinarians to get to the ballroom door. At the end of the hall would be the casino and lobby. He had drunk more than his share of Jack and the constant ringing of slot machines made the pounding in his head worse as he entered the casino. A long walk in the night air would help suppress the pain so he could relax in his room.

Wisemiller's idea that a specific clinic for animal's teeth was ludicrous, he mused as he walked through the casino. The cost of set up would be outrageous, to say the least. If he finds the financial backers he was looking for, he would need to set up in a large city where the customers were more plentiful and willing to pay the astronomical fees. Dental cleaning, for animals was standard procedure every six months, anyway.

He wasn't interested in the money; he enjoyed working with his mom and two older brothers on their quarter horse ranch. He harbored a dream to open a small animal clinic on the property. He didn't have the deal worked out yet, but it was still in his head.

Bells clanged and a woman screamed when her slot machine hit a jackpot. He stepped aside and pressed his thumb and index finger to the bridge of his nose. If he could get away from all the noise and flashing lights, his head might stop throbbing.

The mob of people before him parted and a beautiful woman walked through the opening. Her slow deliberate sway would make any red-blooded male take a second look. His eyes roamed her shapely body. Her legs disappeared under a form fitting black leather dress that clung to every curve. Her sultry, self-assured stride drew him in like a magnet. His perusal reached her face. Her eyes were fixed on him. He met her gaze and her tongue darted out, wetting her bright red lips. Heat burned in his loins.

She continued to stare. Her short, dark hair swished back and forth with every step she took.

The room grew hot. He loosened his tie and unbuttoned the top button of his white shirt. Her eyes bore into him. He smiled to ease his tension and moved over to let her pass. She stepped in front of him.

She walked straight up to him and placed her palms inside his jacket onto his chest.

He gazed down into clear, sky blue eyes. He had plenty of women hit on him before but never in a room full of people. Did he know her? No. He would remember. There were a number of available men in the casino and she had singled him out. He would play her little game.

Her mouth parted seductively. She stood on her tip toes and leaned her head back giving him complete access to her luscious lips. The temptation overwhelmed him. Her hot hand inched around the back of his neck and guided him to her. As soon as his mouth touched hers, she took control. Waves of desire ran through his body like a herd of horses running from a mountain lion. His hand slipped in her leather coat and circled her tiny waist. The room went silent. Or it did in his head. There was just the two of them in the crowded casino. The appeal she generated with that kiss set his blood boiling. He wanted all of her.

She released his mouth slowly and held him captive with her eyes. "Beautiful brown eyes," she murmured. She slid her hand from his neck and tapped the convention badge on his jacket with a long black fingernail. "Justin Garrett, Doctor of Veterinarian Medicine? Are you really a veterinarian?"

Not trusting his voice, he nodded. They were so close he could feel the heat from her body. He inhaled the scent of a very expensive perfume, one he had never smelled before. He liked it, wanted to bury his head in her neck and let her scent intoxicate him.

Her eyes hypnotized him. Her hand on his chest branded an impression on his skin. He placed his hand over hers and squeezed. It shocked him how brazen this beautiful vixen was. He lowered his head, determined to take control. She sighed and returned his advance. He crushed her to his chest. He was oblivious to their surroundings, lost in the passion this woman possessed.

He raised his head. People began to clap. One man yelled, "Get a room."

She chuckled, gave him a slight smile and squeezed his neck. She moved her mouth close to his ear. "I need your services. I'm afraid I've hit a poor animal with my car and it needs attention. Please, can you see if you can help the poor baby? I'll make it worth your time."

He grinned. They did things differently in Vegas. He was more than willing to follow her. Hell, she didn't even need to beg. But one question nagged him. "Why didn't you just ask?"

She cocked her head to one side. "I wanted to convince you."

"I like your form of persuasion." He looked around at several people watching them. "Let's go."

She smiled, released him, and walked ahead into the lobby. Once they were outside, the cold night air hit him. He picked up his step to catch up with her.

"Where's your car?"

She didn't answer but continued to walk at a fast pace to the corner of Tropicana Avenue. A black limousine screeched to a halt at the curb. She opened the front door and climbed inside, slamming the door shut after her.

Two muscular men in black tuxedos got out of the car and sandwiched him between them. One opened the back door. Justin's arms were jerked behind him and secured together with zip ties.

"Hey?" he yelled. A hand quickly covered his mouth and he was shoved into the back seat.

A hood covered his head. He tried to resist but the man had more muscle.

What happened? Was he being abducting? He threw himself over into the man beside him and met with a brick wall. The impact had no effect.

"What the hell is going on?" he demanded.

A hand slapped the side of his head, knocking him over in the seat. "Shut the fuck up, asshole."

The vehicle shot forward. No one spoke.

Chapter 2

The car slowed. A grating noise came from outside and the car moved again. It came to a halt and the engine turned off. The door opened and cool air rushed in. A large hand gripped his arm and pulled him out. The hood was ripped from his head and he blinked several times to focus.

Vehicles lined the stone circle drive. Not just any vehicles but some very expensive Bentleys, a black Jaguar, a bright yellow Lamborghini, and several Cobras. He pressed his lips together. He followed the line of the two-story house next to the drive. The ties binding him were cut and he rubbed his sore wrists. The man shoved him up the steps. The carved wood door swung open and the woman entered. The two men were beside him with their hands on each of his arms.

Loud cheering and yelling came from somewhere in the house.

The woman in the black dress took the stairs to the next level and left him with the two tuxes. As they muscled him through the house the noise grew louder. A wall of French doors stood open revealing a large pool and patio. People dressed in cocktail attire and holding champagne glasses formed a line around the pool area and mingled in groups. He strained to see why they were cheering.

The goons forced him forward away from the party. He glanced over his shoulder. The pool had no water. Red splotches covered the bottom and up the sides of the tile. He heard the growling and barking before he saw the blood-soaked fighting dogs. He gagged and bile rose in his throat. He turned his head away in disgust.

The tux on his left opened the door to a pool house set a few yards away from the party and shoved him inside. Two more men in tuxedos turned when he entered. Behind them, lying on a sheet of plastic, lay a badly injured pit-bull. Blood pooled around the dog, turning the plastic dark red. Several burly men covered in tattoos and wearing leather vests lined the back wall. Each had their tattooed arms crossed in front of their massive chests. A chill ran down his spine. These men could rip him apart with one hand tied behind them.

A heavy-set older man a head shorter than him stepped forward. His eyes narrowed and he removed a half-smoked cigar from his mouth. "Are you a vet?"

Justin tore his eyes away from the injured animal. "Yes."

"I want you to fix this dog. It will be a great loss if he dies."

Justin looked down at the animal. "I'm a large animal doctor. Small animal surgery isn't something I normally do. He stands a better chance at a clinic."

The man stepped closer to him. "You're here and you're a vet. You save the dog and I'll let you go. Do you understand?"

He saw little room for misunderstanding. "I'll do what I can but he's in pretty bad shape so I can't guarantee anything. I don't have surgical instruments or proper medication."

The man walked toward the door. He had his hand on the doorknob and stopped. "Tell Mara what you need and she'll get it for you. If you don't save the dog, then I don't guarantee you'll see tomorrow." The door slammed behind him.

He knelt beside the animal and examined the bite marks. They were deep and blood gushed from the dog's neck. The only sound in the room came from the pit-bull's labored breathing. He pressed his finger to the open wound in hopes of stopping the bleeding. The door opened and closed, followed by footsteps. "I need supplies," he stated to no one in particular.

A soft sultry voice responded. "Make a list."

He glanced at the black leather boots beside him. The woman from the MGM had changed into body hugging leather pants, black tank top, and a black leather vest with Warlords embroidered over her left breast. One snap held the short vest together exposing her mid-section. Her sky blue eyes stared down at him. She leaned over and handed him a tablet with a pen attached.

He quickly jotted down everything he needed and more. The list was long but he didn't want to forget anything. He tore the paper off the tablet and passed it to her. She read over the list and her brow creased.

"Where the fuck am I supposed to get antibiotics, IV, saline, and this other shit? What is a half-moon needle?"

One of the guys against the wall stepped up and placed his large hand on her arm. "In the locked medical cabinet, Mara. Ran's doctor friend furnished the supplies. Come on. I'll show you." She sighed and followed the man out.

He placed his ear against the dog's bloody chest. The heavy pounding concerned him. Thank God he had taken extra classes in treating small animals. The condition of the poor animal was the worst he had ever seen. He didn't hold a lot of hope for him. He looked around at the number of people still gawking at the dog.

"Everyone out. I need privacy and the constant chatter could affect the dog."

Most of the people left but one biker remained. "I'm staying. I can't leave you alone."

Even though his own heart pounded in his chest, Justin's concern now was for his patient. "Fine. Get hot water and clean towels or sheets."

The guy didn't move.

Justin stood and growled his orders. "If you want this dog to have any chance of living, you will do as I say. Now, I need hot water and sterile rags. Tear the rags into strips."

The biker huffed away and returned a few minutes later with a large bowl and several strips of cloth. Justin worked to clean the wounds and pressed the major cut with his hand. He had to get it stitched. Where were those supplies? He listened to the heart again. It was getting weaker.

The door burst open. The woman and other biker entered, their arms loaded with supplies. They dumped the packaged items on the coffee table that had been shoved to one side of the room. Justin searched the items and found one weak antibiotic and filled a syringe, cleaned a spot on the dog, and inserted the needle. He had hoped for the saline bag and painkillers for the dog but he'd have to make do with what he had.

An hour later, all deep cuts had been stitched. He rocked back on his heels. "That's all I can do. We just have to wait and see at this point."

The two bikers stepped forward and took Justin's arms, lifting him from the floor. "You better hope it's enough."

Chapter 3

Mara led the way around the activity still going on in the pool. They entered the main part of the house, and she led the bikers holding Justin between them upstairs. Her stomach wanted to expel the shrimp and caviar she had eaten earlier. All that blood and the needles he had used made her sick. She had kept her head turned most of the time unless he demanded help. Blood covered her arms and all she wanted was a shower.

She had no idea why she kissed him earlier. It wasn't part of the plan. But damn, what a kiss! It had sent heat surging spikes through her. Her body heated above a level she had ever reached in all of her twenty-three years. She wouldn't mind trying that again if he lived beyond sunrise. She unlocked a door and shoved it open.

The biker pushed the vet so hard he fell to his knees. She walked in behind him and helped him up even though he was much taller. But everyone was taller than her five-three height.

"That will be all, Dagger." She shut the door on the biker and walked back to Justin. Her hand grabbed the back of his neck and pulled his head to her. She found his lips and teased them with feather kisses until he responded. He circled her waist, pulled her to his chest and kissed her. Their tongues dueled. A slow burn between her legs sent her body into overdrive. She raised her head, released his neck, and turned to leave.

He grabbed her arm, whirled her around and frowned. "Wait. I did what I could for the dog. Why don't you let me go?"

She hung her head. "I can't. Ran would kill me. One of the Warlords is standing outside the door. You'd never get out alive."

He placed his finger under her chin. She knew if she didn't get out of the room he would see the tears that threatened to spill any minute.

When he spoke she couldn't hold back any longer.

"I don't think you belong with these people." He wiped the tear with his thumb.

She looked into a caring face that at this moment was afraid for his life. She had to play the part she knew so well. "How do you know where I belong? You don't know anything about me."

He ran his fingers through his dark brown hair. "You just seem to be out of place. I saw your face when you looked at the dog. It sickened you."

"I might not like Ran's pastime and it does make me sick but it makes him money. And money makes the world go round." She pressed her back to the wooden door and stared at him.

He stepped closer and leaned his hands on either side pinning her against the door. "Why don't you leave?"

She laughed. "That's a joke. Where would I go? What would I do? Go back to stripping for pennies? I don't think so."

His brown eyes bore in to her. "I can help you, Mara. Is that what I heard the guy call you?"

"Yes, it's Mara and you're crazy." She twisted and opened the door. She was out before he could say anything else. She locked the door and went to her room. She had seen enough for one night.

She hated the dog fights. There was always too much blood and too many senseless animal deaths. Once she had voiced her disapproval to Ran. After he used her for a punching bag, she never mentioned the fights again. She attended the events because he demanded that she be present. She unzipped her boots and peeled the leather pants and vest off. She turned the water on in the shower and pulled the tank top over her head. The hot water soothed her tired body. She raised her head and let the rain shower cover her face and head. Raniero would not be happy she hadn't come back to the party. He expected her to be the perfect hostess for the length of the fights. They usually lasted until dawn. It was after two now and she was past exhausted. His wrath could wait until later. He hadn't hit her since putting her in the hospital, but he had demands. One being that she had to sleep in the nude. That was fine with her. She didn't like to be inhibited when she slept.

She shampooed the smoke and dog stink from her hair and turned the water off. After using the fluffy towel on her body, she dried her hair and crawled under the bright yellow comforter. Sleep evaded her despite her fatigue. When she closed her eyes, she saw the handsome doctor. His expert hands had worked on the animal tirelessly. She had picked the right veterinarian. Ran would be happy about that.

Why did she kiss him again? Maybe she wanted to see if he set off the sparks she had experienced in the casino. He had all right. If there wasn't a house full of people she would have fucked him. There might be another chance. If the dog lived.

The banging on her door startled her. She grabbed her robe from the foot of the bed and went to let them in.

Dagger's brow sat low over his eyes. "Demon's dead."

Chapter 4

Justin went into the bathroom and stripped. He cleaned up as best he could and put the blood stained clothes back on. He sat down on the bed. His elbows pressed into his knees and he rested his head in his palms. The dog wasn't going to make it. He had done everything he could but knew it wasn't enough. There was internal bleeding. He got the bleeding in his neck stopped and tried attaching the vein before applying stitches but he didn't have the equipment needed for such a precise surgery.

He wanted to see if the woman would help him escape. She didn't give him a chance to ask. They had connected though. As much passion as they generated with just a kiss, there wasn't any doubt. What did she see in these people? Had Ran been the man giving orders in the pool house? Could she be in love with him or his money? He knew he was right. She didn't belong here. There had to be a way to convince her.

"Who the hell are you kidding?" She wouldn't be here if she didn't want to be.

There had to be a way out, with or without Mara. Somehow he didn't think money would faze them. What would his brothers do? Both being lawmen they would devise a plan and execute it. He was a doctor and didn't have that type of knowledge. He fell back on the comforter. His only option was the woman.

An hour later and unable to sleep, he went into the bathroom and splashed cold water on his face. He shut the faucet off and heard the key in the door. He stepped back into the bedroom and Mara stood in the door with two bikers behind her.

"You need to come with us." She wouldn't meet his eyes as Dagger and Rummy manhandled him out the door.

They escorted him down the stairs and past the empty patio. Dark red blood covered the bottom of the pool. His stomach retched and he gagged. He slowed but the men pushed him toward the pool house. Once inside he glanced at the floor where he had worked on the pit. The dog was gone. All the medical supplies had been cleared away and the room didn't look like it had been an operating room. The man, who might be Ran, stood in the middle of the room. The bikers held Justin's arms and stopped in front of the older man.

"The dog died. You could have saved him. I don't need your services any longer." He started to leave and stopped when Justin spoke.

"A major artery had been severed. I tried to repair it but didn't have the convenience of an operating room and special equipment it would take. I'm not the one who didn't save him." His hands doubled into fists. Blood rushed to his head. "You, sir, can only blame yourself for the dog's death."

A fist punched Justin in his kidneys and he fell forward, landing on the coffee table. He rolled off and stood. The same guy hit him on his jaw. A chair kept him from hitting the floor. Blood seeped into his mouth. His head spun and his vision blurred.

"Get rid of him." The older man ordered and left.

The bikers lifted him and his eyes met Mara's. She frowned and left the room. They held his arms and ushered him out the front of the mansion. They shoved him into the limo and one of the men slipped in beside him. The other went around to the driver's side and started the vehicle.

The lights of the city disappeared. They weren't going back into Vegas. His heart tried to jump out of his chest. He eased a hand over to the door handle and pulled. Locked. His only chance would be to try to get away when they stopped. He had to clear his head and think. He had keys and a little change in his pocket. His dress shoes wouldn't make a good weapon but they were better than nothing.

The limo left the highway. They bumped over a rough dirt road and came to rest in a clearing. The guy next to him opened the door and jerked Justin out. As soon as he had his feet on the ground, he ran. The biker tackled him from behind and his face buried in the sand. He grabbed a handful of dirt. The man pulled him to his feet and Justin slung the grit in his face.

The big guy sputtered and spit and rubbed his eyes.

"You motherfucker!" He smashed his fist into Justin's ribs. He grabbed his side and bent over. The man kneed him in the face and Justin fell backwards. He rolled over and a heavy boot kicked him in the ribs. He grabbed his side, now burning with pain. The larger man jumped on him, pinning his arms with his knees, and hit him repeatedly in the head. Blood gushed from his mouth and nose. His teeth cut into his jaw and an agonizing pain shot through his face. The biker wouldn't stop. He grabbed his arm, put his boot on top, and twisted. Justin screamed when the arm cracked.

"That's enough, Dagger. Just shoot him and get it over with," the other one yelled.

He climbed off of Justin and reached for something behind him. "Shit. I dropped my gun." He kicked at the ground searching for the missing weapon.

Justin blinked, trying to focus through the blood running into his eyes. He forced his broken arm into his right hand, scrambled to his feet and ran. A gun fired and a piercing pain shot through his shoulder. He fell to his knees and crawled under a dense plant covered in thorns that cut into his exposed skin.

Chapter 5

"He's getting away. Get him."

Justin caught a second wind and ran toward the cover of some boulders. He climbed over a small hill and realized, too late, the rocks bordered a ravine on the other side. He tumbled into the dark ditch. The sun was beginning to rise but shadows from the sides of the ravine kept it dark at the bottom. He lay flat and waited.

"You lost him."

"I didn't lose him, you did. You were supposed to be watching. I think I shot him."

Boots clomped around on the loose rock above him. He held his breath and didn't move. The men were at the edge of the ravine.

Something crawled across his hand and onto his chest. He tensed but kept still.

"Shit. Let's get out of here before the sun comes up. I've been up since yesterday and I'm tired."

"You idiot. We have to make sure he's dead or it's our necks."

"Fine. You stick around and make sure. I'm leaving." The footsteps faded. A moment later the other man followed.

He raised his head to see a large black tarantula resting on his blood-stained shirt. He swatted it away and tried to sit up. His body wouldn't cooperate. He bit his lip to keep from crying out. He needed a doctor. He suffered the climb to the top of the ravine and found shelter under a huge rock that jutted away from the hill. If he could rest for a few minutes he might be able to make it back to the road. Sledge hammers were beating inside his head. He spit blood and struggled to breath. The stinging in his shoulder throbbed and his chest hurt with every breath. He could have a punctured lung. He was going to die.

***

Mara saw the limo enter the highway and head back toward town. She started her Harley and pulled onto the dirt road. The loose sand caused the bike to slip but she kept it in control. She spotted the clearing and parked. The morning sun provided enough light to follow the footprints to the ravine. She had to find him and see what kind of damage they had inflicted. If he was even alive.

She examined the ground and saw the crawl marks over the bikers' boot prints. She smiled. He was alive. She walked the path made by the drag marks that ended at some boulders. He had to be here somewhere. She hoped she wasn't too late. She climbed over a rock and saw him lying in the shade afforded by a giant rock. He wasn't moving. She scooted down the rock, crawled underneath, and pressed her hand to his chest. He had a heartbeat.

"Justin, wake up." She took the bottle of water from her backpack and raised it to his lips. He spurted and swung his hand at her. "Easy there, cowboy. I'm here to help. Sip." She raised the bottle again. He obliged. His eyes were almost swollen shut and a stream of dried blood formed a line from his nose.

She took a rag out of her pack, wet it, and wiped at the blood. "What hurts?"

Brown eyes peeped between his swollen lids.

"Everything," he managed through parched lips.

"Well, I'm not in the medical field so you need to be more specific. I have a first-aid kit on the bike but I think you need more than a Band-Aid."

He reached for the bottle and drank. He moaned as he tried to sit up. He fell back against the sand and touched the lump on the side of his face. "They shot me. I think my nose and arm are broken. Can you take me to a hospital?"

She rocked back on her boots. "I don't think that would be a good idea. Ran has people everywhere. He would know where to find you before you could see a doctor. I have another idea. Can you get up?"

He rolled over and pulled his knees up under his stomach. With his good arm, he pushed his upper body away from the ground. She grabbed his arm and he yelped.

"Sorry." She wrapped her arm around his back and pulled him out from under the ledge.

He grabbed a rock and lifted himself into a standing position. He slipped his good arm around her shoulder and hobbled down the hill.

She knew it was a long walk back to the bike. "Stop for a minute and rest."

"I'm okay." She had to strain to hear his weak voice.

They reached the bike and she released him. She unlocked the saddlebag, pulled out a red and black helmet and handed it to him. "Here. Put this on." She strapped her matching helmet on and looked at him. He had gotten the hood on but couldn't connect the straps. "Let me do that."

"Why are you doing this?"

"What?" She finished hooking the strap and swung her leg over the bright orange Harley.

He waved his good hand. "This. Helping me."

She smiled at him. "I like the way you kiss." She lowered her visor. "Get on."

It took time but he finally managed to get on the motorcycle. When his hand touched her bare skin, she shivered. He was holding on but it felt more like a caress. Her lower region throbbed. Damn, what this man did to her!

He cried out every time the bike hit a rut. She dodged most but couldn't miss them all. Once they got to the paved highway, the ride got easier. He laid his head on her shoulder. His hot body pressed against her back sent desire through her.

They reached Las Vegas city limits. She stayed off the main strip and wove the bike through back streets. She came to a halt in front of The Pink Titty. Flashing pink and purple lights lit up the front with neon signs of half-naked women.

"Leave the helmet on." She didn't want anyone to see his bruised and battered face. She threw her leather jacket around his shoulders and lifted the collar. He leaned against her as they walked inside. Colored lights flashed on the half nude woman on the stage making suggestive dance moves around a pole to *Let's Get it On* by Marvin Gaye. The sour odors of hundreds of spilled drinks and male bodies turned her stomach. Memories of the hours she had spent taking her clothes off and dancing around that pole and having sweaty hands paw at her body sickened her. She would still be here if Ran hadn't made his seemingly fairy-tale offer.

"Mara. What brings you back?" A large guy who could double as a wrestler caressed her cheek. "We've missed you around here."

She turned her head away from his hand. "My friend wants special treatment and I told him I knew just the place. Is Dixie working tonight?"

"Dixie works every night." He looked over his shoulder. "She may be on break. Go on back."

"He wants to pay for the blue light room. With all the trimmings, of course. Is it still two hundred?"

"It is for you."

She fished two one hundred dollar bills from her hip pocket and handed them to him. He turned to lead the way. "Don't bother. I know the way. Can you get Dixie?" He started to walk off and she stopped him. "Tell her he wants the pink sequin bag."

The bouncer grinned. "Will do." He walked around the tables and disappeared behind the stage curtains.

She helped him to the back of the club and opened a door to the room she knew so well. It had been a little over two years since she had been here and the unpleasant memories flooded back. It hadn't been a mistake to accept Raniero's offer. He had rescued her from this despicable situation that she hated so. Perhaps, she mused as she lay Justin on the large blue sofa and removed the helmet, she had gone from the frying pan into the fire. Well, at least she had drawn the line with Ran's suggestion that she service his elite friends.

The door swung open and a tall blonde wearing black pasties with tassels hanging from each breast and a G-string entered. "Mara." She grabbed the younger girl and hugged her. "I sure didn't expect to see you here again."

"It's great to see you, Dixie. I wouldn't be here if it wasn't an emergency." She held her friend's arm and turned her toward Justin. "This is a friend of mine and he needs medical attention. You know why I can't take him to the emergency room. It's just too risky."

"I understand. Now, tell me what's going on. I can see he's in pretty bad shape."

Mara sat on the sofa next to him. "He's a veterinarian. There's a convention in town."

Dixie raised her brows and nodded. "Boy, do I know it. We've had several in here. So what happened to him?"

"Ran sent me after a vet to save Demon. I found him walking through the casino."

"Let me guess. The dog died and his goons beat the crap out of him then dumped him in the desert."

She nodded. "Something like that. He's been shot but I think it went through. His arm may be broke and he's complaining about his chest hurting when he breathes."

Dixie opened her bag and took out several instruments. "Doc, tell me where you hurt."

"I know my left arm is broken and my shoulder hurts where he shot me but I think it's a through and through. I thought a rib had punctured a lung but I'm breathing better so it may be cracked. My nose is broken and I may need stitches in a couple of places." He ran his hand across his face and cringed when he touched the bridge of his nose.

"They really did a number on you. You should be in the ER but I understand why you aren't. Let me get your vitals, check that bullet wound, sew up the cuts, and then I want to examine the ribs. We'll set the arm last."

He moaned as he rolled over on his side. "I need a real doctor. No offense to you, Ma'am."

Dixie continued to thread sutures. "Don't worry, doc. I'm a fourth year medical student and this ain't my first rodeo. Now, let's get that shirt off."

They helped him sit up and Dixie examined the hole in his shoulder.

"The wound in your shoulder is a low velocity injury with no bone involvement or non-operative fractures. That's good news. It has stopped bleeding and I think a couple of stitches in front and back will take care of it. It has a nice clean entry and exit. Must have used a small caliber on you. This is going to burn a little." She poured a liquid on both holes. His hand clenched the sheet and he groaned. She put two stitches in front then in back.

"Let's do the ribs next. You may pass out when we set the arm."

Dixie's fingers moved over his ribcage. "I think a few may be cracked, but not broke. They'll heal themselves in about four weeks. Coughing and moving is going to be painful." She looked at Mara. "Antibiotics use in this case is a bit controversial, especially since I gave him a tetanus but I'd rather be safe than sorry. Can you get him an oral antibiotic?"

"I can try."

"Something is better than nothing. While you're at it, get Percocet, Demerol, or Tylenol 3 for pain. Okay, handsome, let's set that arm. This is going to hurt like a motha." She slipped her spiked heels off and placed a foot on the bed and picked up Justin's limp arm. "Ready?"

He nodded. Dixie snapped the bone back in place with one quick jerk. He cried out and fell silent.

Chapter 5

"Okay, buddy. Time to go."

He opened his eyes and cringed when the burly bouncer pulled on his arm. Mara placed the leather coat over his shoulders and opened the door. The man put Justin's good arm around his neck and helped him out a side door where a taxi waited.

"Thanks, Bo." She stood on her tiptoes and kissed the big guy on the cheek. He shut the car door after the couple were inside. "Motel 8 on Tropicana."

"Where's the bike?" Justin asked.

"I didn't think you were in any shape to ride it. Dixie will take care of it for me."

The cabbie made several turns and got on the strip. Traffic was heavy but he weaved in and out turning on Tropicana and finally pulled into the motel. She handed him a few bills and they got out.

She walked him into the shade away from the motel windows. "You wait here. I'll get the room."

She returned a few minutes later and helped him to room one forty-six. The musty odor hit him when he stepped through the door. He really didn't care as long as he could lay down. She threw her backpack on the bed close to the bathroom and he sunk onto the other.

His suit was ruined and all his clothes were at the MGM Grand. He wanted to get the dried blood off and hoped the water would soothe his soreness. "I'd like to wash off. Is there anything I can cover the shoulder wound with so it doesn't get wet?"

"Maybe we can tape the shower cap over it. Give me twenty minutes and I'll be back to help you."

He strained to turn around. "Where are you going?"

"To get your medicine and some tape."

He frowned. "Without a prescription?"

Her eyebrows rose.

"Oh." She didn't intend to get it legally. If he had his pad he would write a prescription. That was also in his hotel room. "Wouldn't we be more comfortable in a nicer hotel?"

"That's the first place they'll look. The boss always wants proof that the guys have done what they were supposed to do. They usually cut off a finger. He'll send them back to the desert to make sure you're dead. Then they'll start looking." She grabbed her bag off the bed and went to the door. "Don't open this for anyone but me." The door slammed behind her.

He maneuvered to the head of the bed and lay on the pillow. Exhaustion overcame him and he fell asleep.

***

Mara knew where she needed to go. Three blocks down Tropicana and left on Chips. She should find everything she needed on the street. She walked until she spotted the slow moving red Mustang and stepped into the street. The car pulled alongside her. She leaned on the door.

She recognized one of the men in the car. "Hey guys. I need some pain meds. I also need some Mr. Blue. Do you know where I can get them?"

"You using again, Mara?"

"No. I have a friend who got the shit beat out of him and he's hurting pretty bad. You got any or not?"

"Don't get your panties in a wad. I gotcha covered." He reached over the seat, retrieved a bag, and dug inside. He held up two plastic bags. "Here ya go. I don't normally carry antibiotics but there's been a lot of people here lately who don't want to go to no hospital. I say, to each his own."

"How much?"

"Hundred. Just for old time's sake."

She handed him two fifties, took the bags, and walked away.

She looked over her shoulder and as soon as the Mustang was out of sight, she hailed a cab. "Galleria at Sunset."

She entered an exclusive store and went to the cosmetic department; picked up a bottle of expensive body wash, shampoo and strolled over to the men's section.

An associate approached. "May I help you?"

"I need underwear, jeans, socks, and a couple of shirts."

"Certainly. What size?"

She rubbed the back of her neck. "He's at least six-three and weights about one-seventy-five."

The clerk smiled. "I think I can work with that. If they don't fit, you can always bring them back."

After finding her own size in jeans and shirts she paid with the gift card Ran had given her for her birthday last year. She left the store and walked two blocks to a drugstore and picked up bandages, antiseptic, plastic wrap, and duct tape. On the way to checkout she grabbed several protein bars and a couple of sodas. Outside she found a cab and went back to the hotel. He had passed out on the bed. Even in the bloodstained clothes he had to be the best looking man she had ever seen. He stirred when she placed her hand to his forehead. He wasn't hot, which, she supposed, was a good sign. She put the meds beside the bed and went into the bathroom and turned on the shower.

She went back and sat on the bed. "Justin."

His eyes opened. They were swollen and bloodshot. She ached for him.

"The shower is warm. Let's get that gunshot wound taped so you can get cleaned up."

She slipped the shirt off and covered the wound with Saran wrap, securing it with duct tape. He tried to sit up and moaned. She shook two pain pills from the bag and handed them to him with a glass of water. After he took the pills, she reached for his good arm. "Take my hand and pull yourself up."

In the bathroom he had trouble getting undressed with one hand. She sighed and took his clothes off. His battered and bruised body was firm to her touch. She fought the urge to run her fingers over every muscle. She wanted him, even now when he was so obviously in pain. Her tongue darted out and licked her lips. She ran her hands slowly up his chest and gazed into his swollen eyes. He placed his hand on her cheek and lowered his head, capturing her lips.

Bolts of lightning shot through her. Their tongues tied together.

He raised his head. "Join me."

She glanced at the tiny tub. "I don't think we'll both fit in that."

"We can try."

She slipped the leather vest off and pulled the tank over her head. She reached for the clasp of her black lace bra and he stopped her.

He slipped his hand around to her back. "I can do this one handed."

She kicked off her boots and peeled out of the leather pants. He stepped into the tub, under the warm water. She climbed in and shut the plastic curtain closed. She eased into his arm and circled his neck with her hands. He kissed her hungrily. This was an emotional high she had never had before and there had been plenty of opportunity. Why? What made this time different? How could this one man pull from her something no other man had?

He lowered his hand to her breast and took the sensitive nipple between his thumb and index finger and massaged it gently. Fire shot straight down her body and settled between her legs. She burned for him. She took his erect member in her hand and teased while the water covered them both. It was like an aphrodisiac tingling sensitive parts of their hot bodies. He lowered his hand and found her hot spot and slipped a finger inside. Her head fell back and she moaned. He covered her throat with kisses and moved his finger slowly kindling the flame already burning.

"Tell me where you want to go, Mara. I'll take you there."

She had never been asked that before. It had never been about what she wanted but all about what they wanted. Ran had lost the ability to perform over a year ago and she had been celibate since. His loss of interest didn't hurt her feelings any. She never got anything out of it anyway. But this man had awakened places in her that had never been awake.

"I want to fuck you."

"Sorry. You can't do that. But you can let me make love to you." He leaned his head against her forehead. "I promise you won't be disappointed."

Shock overwhelmed her. No one had ever made love to her before. She pressed her back to the wall, pulling him to her, she wrapped her legs around his waist. She guided his cock to her and inserted the tip. He groaned. She froze. "Did I hurt you?"

"Oh no. You are so hot. It's wonderful." He put his arm under her bare butt and eased into her. He started a slow rhythm then picked up the pace and shoved deeper. She matched his strokes. She loved it and the heat building in her lower body took her by surprise. Before long she knew she was headed for the very first climax she had ever had and she let it happen. They reached the peak at the same time. "Justin." She couldn't help but call his name when she came.

Their heavy breathing subsided and she lowered her legs. He eased out of her but didn't let her go. He found her lips and kissed her deeply. "You are amazing."

She was speechless. His words sunk in and she disagreed. "No, you were."

When they both recovered, she bathed him and he did the same to her with one hand. "Are you hurting?" She asked.

"Surprisingly, no." He wrapped a towel around his waist and kissed her. "I feel wonderful."

She grinned and removed the plastic from his shoulder. "I bought you some clothes. I hope they fit."

He dropped the towel, giving her a full view of his gorgeous body. There wasn't an ounce of fat on him anywhere, unlike Ran. Gingerly she removed the plastic wrap from his shoulder. He slipped into the briefs and crawled under the covers. She threw on one of the t-shirts she bought and pulled the cover back on the other bed.

"Are you sleeping over there?" He asked.

"I thought I would."

"Sleep with me, please."

She sat next to him, handed him two protein bars and popped the top of one of the sodas. She opened the Ziploc bag. "Eat those bars and then take these two pills."

"What are they?"

"Antibiotics. You can't take them on an empty stomach"

He devoured the bars and swallowed the pills. She crawled in beside him. He pulled her into his arms.

"Tell me about where you live."

"It's one of the most beautiful ranches in East Texas. We have about four thousand acres and raise and train quarter horses."

"Does the ranch have a name?"

"Garrett Quarter Horses. It belongs to my two brothers, Carson and Rex, my mother, and me."

She caressed his day-old stubble. "Do you all live together?"

He shook his head. "We each have our own homes. Three of the log homes are exactly alike and Rex just built a larger log home up on the mountain. Mom and Jamie, Rex's wife, raise pygmy goats and they are the cutest little guys."

"Did you always want to be a veterinarian?"

"I guess it has been a given that I become a vet. The more I studied, the more I liked it. I like working with the horses but I love the small animals better. I would like to open a clinic for small animals someday."

They were silent and she realized the long day, pain pills, and warm shower had taken effect. She listened to his even breathing and was thankful the medication was strong enough to relax him. She closed her eyes and sleep came a lot sooner than it had in a long time.

Chapter 6

Justin opened his eyes and he had to think for a minute to remember where he was. He moved and pain shot through his shoulder, ribs, and arm, reminding him. It all came flooding back. She turned over, releasing his arm, giving him the freedom to get up and go to the bathroom. When he returned she was sitting against the headboard. Her nipples were taunt under the tight t-shirt she wore. She was more beautiful without the dark eye make-up.

"You look inviting."

She grinned and threw the cover back, revealing tanned, shapely legs. He slipped out of his briefs and crawled in next to her. He ran his hand across her flat stomach and raised her shirt. He took a hardened nipple into his mouth. She scooted down and feathered her fingers through his hair. He hadn't expected her to be gentle in love making considering where she came from. He lowered his hand and massaged her v-zone.

"Oh, Justin. That is wonderful."

He slipped his finger inside and she groaned. She was wet. He put another finger inside and moved slowly. Her hips followed his movement. His cock throbbed. She circled it with her fingers and took it in her hand.

"I wanted this to be slower than the first time but I'm not sure I can wait."

"You really turn me on. I'm okay with not waiting but I want on top." She increased the massage and he wanted to burst. She eased him over onto his back and straddled him. With expert hands, she guided him inside and took all of him with one thrust. He was on fire.

Before long they climbed together over the edge of the most amazing sexual encounter he had ever experienced. She collapsed against his chest, breathing heavily. He rubbed her back until they recovered. She rolled off and lay next to him. He covered her with his arm and kissed her cheek.

"I think I could get used to this."

"Did you mean what you said about helping me get away from here?"

He leaned up on his elbow and looked into her clear blue eyes. "I never say things I don't mean."

"When were you supposed to leave?"

"What day is it?"

"Saturday."

"My flight is tomorrow."

She faced him. "I want to go with you."

He kissed her. "I'd like that, a lot. Where is your family?"

She inhaled and blew it out slowly. "I don't have family. I've been in foster homes most of my life."

"You don't know where your mom and dad are?"

She nodded. "Oh, sure. My dad is in prison and my mom overdosed when I was three. When I was seventeen the foster family kicked me out and I lived on the streets for a year. Surviving any way I could."

He pulled her to him. "I'm so sorry. You need a new start and moving to Texas might be just the thing."

Her eyes clouded. "Ran took me out of the strip joint but his kindness didn't last." She blinked away her sadness. "I'm hungry. Let's go get something to eat. Do you feel like walking?"

She didn't want to talk about her past. He could wait until she was ready. "I think the physical therapy you gave me last night and this morning has put me on the mend." He looked around the tiny room. "Where's my suit?"

***

She took the new clothes out of the bag and handed them to him. "I hope they fit."

Her panties got wet at the sight of how well his tight butt and muscular legs filled out the Levi's. But when he slipped the honey brown Polo over his head it looked like someone had tinted the shirt to match his eyes. He took her breath away.

She stood in her black thong staring at him.

"Are you going without clothes?"

She turned her back and tore off the tags of the jeans she bought for herself.

"That's an unusual tattoo. What is it?" He remarked.

She grabbed her butt cheek. She had forgotten about it. "Something Ran insisted I get. He said it's Greek and represents his devotion to me. What a joke." She fastened the black bra and slipped into the jeans. The navy top went over her head; leaving the half zipper open revealing a good portion of her breast. Her black knee-high boots fit over the jeans perfectly. She handed him a baseball cap she bought and put another on her head.

They left the room and walked the two blocks to the 50's Diner. The place was full and they had to sit at the counter. She didn't like being in full view of anyone coming in but there wasn't another choice. He ordered coffee and she had orange juice.

"Tell me about yourself. I know you live in Texas but where?"

He doctored his coffee with cream and sugar and sipped. "I live halfway between Dallas and Shreveport on the outskirts of Tyler."

"Do you…" She felt the blood rush from her face. In the mirror behind the counter she saw two familiar faces enter. She pulled the cap down and lowered her head.

He leaned closer. "Is something wrong?"

"Two of the Warlords just walked in. They'll recognize me. We have to get out of here."

"They don't know me. You leave and I'll get the food to go."

"Mara. What are you doing here? I didn't see your bike outside." One of the bikers patted her on the back.

She swiveled around. "It's in the shop for an oil change." She slid off the stool. "I was just leaving, Badger. I have an appointment." She rushed out the door and hurried down the street, slipping into the shadow of an empty building. Her breath came in short pants and perspiration beaded on her forehead. She clasped her shaking hands together and peeked around the corner.

Her insides quivered. Sweat ran down between her breasts as she waited. A few minutes later Justin walked by. She grabbed his arm and pulled him into the shadows. "Did anyone follow you?"

"No. I don't think they knew we were together."

She pulled him toward the motel. "Don't kid yourself. They know everything."

Once inside the room, she parted the curtains and looked up and down the street.

"They're not coming, Mara. Come eat."

She had lost her appetite and shoved the food around on the Styrofoam plate. Ran knew she was gone by now. The bikers had to be searching for her. They had to get out of the motel. She shoved a fork of eggs into her mouth and heard the loud roar of motorcycles. She jumped up and peeked through the curtains. Five bikers drove down slowly down the street.

"We have to leave."

"Let's go to the airport. I'll change my flight and purchase another ticket. We can be out of Nevada on the next plane."

She nodded and called a cab. Ten minutes later they heard the horn blow outside and rushed from the room and into the cab. "McCarran International," she instructed. The vehicle pulled out of the motel parking lot.

They arrived at the busy airport and she covered her mouth with her hand. Four Harleys were parked at the loading and unloading ramp. They sat in the no parking section. Bikers did whatever they wanted. The Warlords could be very intimidating.

She leaned over the front seat. "I've changed my mind. Take us to the MGM Grand."

"What are you doing?"

"They're here. We can't get out. They're watching the airport. I need to think. There will be lots of people at the Grand and we'll be less likely to get abducted from such a busy place."

His eyebrows creased together. "More people than the airport? There's security here."

She nodded. "It doesn't matter. Ran has people everywhere. They'll get by the guards without anyone knowing."

The cab drove back to the MGM and Justin paid the driver. They entered the lobby and he went to the registration desk.

"Justin Garrett in room twelve-eighty. I've misplaced my key-card."

"Could I see your ID, please?"

He produced his driver's license from his wallet and the clerk gave him a new card. "Mr. Garrett, are you still checking out in the morning?"

"Will it be a problem if I decide to stay a few more days?"

The clerk clicked keys on the computer. "No, sir. We might have to move you to another room. There are several tour buses coming in tonight and tomorrow and they have requested a number of rooms on that floor. Would you mind moving now?"

"No problem." He waited for the clerk to assign him another room and a new room key.

"I'll have the bellman move your things." He pressed the bell on the counter and a bellboy approached. "We are moving Mr. Garrett to eleven-ten. Please move his luggage to the new room."

Justin took her hand and led her to the elevator. The bellman punched twelve. They entered the room and loaded his things into his suit cases. The man took the bags and led them to the elevator.

Eleven-ten was a nicer suite with a larger bathroom and king size bed. The bellman put the bags on a table bedside the door and Justin tipped him.

"This is nice." She passed the bed and walked to the large window overlooking the strip. He stepped up behind her.

"This is a bonus. I didn't expect this view. I bet it's beautiful after dark." He slipped an arm around her shoulder. "Are you hungry since we didn't get to finish our breakfast?"

She leaned her head against his shoulder. "I don't think it's a good idea for us to venture out again."

He dropped his arm and entered the bedroom. "We'll get room service." He picked up the phone and ordered two rib eyes, baked potatoes, chef salads, and a bottle of Merlot.

He needed a plan. He sat on the end of the bed. They had to get out of this town. But how?

With the airport being staked out by the gang it wouldn't be easy to slip by them. He could call home and have Carson or Rex fly the company jet into a private airport. He rubbed the back of his neck. Involving his brothers didn't appeal to him.

The bed pressed down beside him and she laid a hand on his arm. "What are you thinking so hard about?"

"How to get out of Vegas. I think we should rent a car and drive to Texas."

She shot up and threw her arms in the air. "Are you serious? Do you think Ran wouldn't know about a rental before we got to the city limits? He has informers everywhere. They'll follow us."

"He won't follow us to Texas."

She shook her head. "You don't know him. He'll come after me where ever I go. I know too much."

"You'll be safe on the ranch," he argued.

"I don't know. I need to think."

A knock at the door interrupted their debate. "Room service."

Chapter 7

She awoke to the sound of sirens in the street. She glanced at him as he slept peacefully. She wrapped a blanket around her naked body and walked to the window. Four police cars and two ambulances sat in front of the Grand. The uniformed people below moved in and out of the hotel. Paramedics wheeled two gurneys out and drove away, sirens blaring.

She stepped back and clenched the blanket tighter to steady her shaking hands. Wild geese were flying around in her stomach. Something wasn't right. It might have been a heart attack victim but she didn't think so. Slipping into her jeans and shirt she grabbed the room key and eased into the hall. She didn't know why it was so important for her to know what was going on but she had to ease her mind.

In the lobby she headed to the concierge.

"May I help you?"

"Can you tell me what happened this morning? I saw the police and ambulance. My family was due in last night. I haven't heard from them and I can't get them on the phone." It was the only thing she could think of.

"What is your family's name?"

She gave the first name that came to mind. Her last foster parents'. "Gorman."

He shook his head. "It wasn't them." He continued to work on the computer.

She reached across the counter and put her hand on his arm. "Please, what happened?"

The clerk looked over his shoulder and leaned over the counter. "Someone broke into twelve-eighty and attacked the two people staying there."

Her body turned cold. She wrapped her arms around her waist. "Will they be all right?"

He shrugged his shoulders as another man walked up beside him. That was all she would get from the clerk.

She rushed to the elevator and punched eleven. When she walked in the room, Justin came out of the bathroom and kissed her cheek. "Where've you been?"

She couldn't breathe. Her hand went to her neck. She gasped and tried to get the words out but it was difficult. "Twelve-eighty…attack…people…hurt."

He pulled her to the bed and forced her to sit. "Mara, calm down. Breathe and tell me what happened."

A loud knock on the door startled her. "They're here." She grabbed the front of his shirt.

He started toward the door and she pulled him back. "No. It's the gang."

"Mr. Garrett, this is the police. Open up, please."

She released him, stood, and covered her mouth with her hand. He opened the door. Two officers in suits stood in the hall, holding their badges up for examination.

"Is something wrong?" he asked.

"May we come in?" The tallest officer stepped forward, not waiting for an answer. "I understand you were staying in room twelve-eighty and the hotel moved you late yesterday."

"Yes. What's this about?"

The man ignored his question. "Do you know of anyone who has a grudge against you?" He looked around Justin at Mara, "or the young lady?"

Her heart jumped into her throat and beat loud in her ears.

Justin didn't answer right away. He ran his hand through his hair. "Not to my knowledge."

"I believe you were in town for the veterinary convention that ended yesterday. Is that correct?" The other officer took notes on a small pad.

"Yes. I decided to stay for a few days and take in the sights. Can you tell me why all the questions?"

"Someone broke into the room you were staying in last night. The couple was attacked. Nothing was stolen that we could tell so we're exploring the possibilities the attack was meant for another person. Since you were the last person to have that room, we're just checking."

"I don't believe anyone in the area knows me."

"Looks like you got into a pretty bad scrape. How did you get the bruises and broken arm?"

Most of his injuries were covered by his shirt. She hoped they didn't notice her trembling body.

"My girlfriend has a motorcycle and we hit a pothole and lost control."

The taller officer looked at her. "How come you didn't sustain any injuries, ma'am?"

A lump formed in her throat and her mouth was dry as the desert. She rubbed her tongue against the roof of her mouth. "He grabbed me so I fell on top of him."

"Did you file a police report?"

They weren't going to give up. What was a good reason not to file a report? She didn't have to come up with one. Justin did it for her.

"She was driving and already has two accidents on her insurance. She didn't want another so I just paid for the repairs."

"Where is the bike now?"

She stepped up beside him and held his arm. "At the repair shop. Somewhere on Fremont."

The officer taking notes looked over his glasses and raised his eyebrows. He flipped his pad closed. "That will be all for now. Are you planning to leave any time soon?"

"We were thinking about leaving today." Justin said.

"Let me have your phone numbers in case we have any more questions."

He gave the detective his number and the ranch number. Mara had left her phone at the house. "I don't have a phone. I rely on him." She told the officer.

"You can reach her through me."

After the police left he took her in his arms. "You're shaking. I guess I need to contact my brother."

"What can he do from Texas?"

"He's an FBI agent."

She jerked her head up from his chest. "Your brother is with the FBI? I thought your family had a ranch."

"We do. Rex can contact the agency here in Vegas. You said you couldn't trust anyone. With Rex's help we can tell the FBI what we know and get out of town."

That wasn't going to work. She strolled over to the bed. "They'll need proof and we don't have anything but our word. But I know where to get everything we need."

He turned her around. "What are you thinking, Mara? Ran's goons may have already killed two innocent people and they won't stop until they find us. I won't let you go back to that house."

"I don't have to. The records are at his construction office. Under the desk in a hidden compartment. I worked there for a short time until Ran got jealous of the men hitting on me. I know how to bypass the security system. I can pick the lock on the gate and door to the office. The only thing I don't know how to do is get past the Dobermans. There are four and they are trained to attack."

He grinned. "I can take care of the animals. What about guards?"

"He may have a guard posted but I doubt it. He's using all the bikers to search for me. Besides, he doesn't think I'm smart enough to steal from him. I can get in, get the jump drives that list all of his activities, bank accounts, and names. They will be all the FBI needs."

"I don't know, baby. It sounds easy but what if something goes wrong, we have no back-up plan and no one in Vegas we can trust. Shouldn't we contact the FBI first?"

She put her arms around his neck. "The FBI is not going to listen to the ex-girlfriend of a mob boss. We have to get the records. We can do this."

He pulled her closer. "First thing we need to do is check out of this hotel and find another place to stay."

"I think so, too. I'll gather our things and we'll leave."

Chapter 8

When they checked out of the hotel Justin asked the concierge for the address of the nearest car rental. Outside they found a cab in front of the Grand.

He helped her in and gave the cabbie the address. "Twenty-four hundred Grand Avenue."

They stopped a few minutes later in front of the car rental and the driver turned in the seat. "Twelve dollars and eighty cents."

Justin paid the fee and they went inside to rent a car. He got behind the wheel of a white Camry. "Where to?"

"Take a left on Fremont Avenue at the next red light. We're going to the Desert View. It's about three miles outside of town."

He followed her directions and spotted the flashing sign at the motel. It was off the main stream of the strip. The sign below Desert View read Specialty Themed Rooms. He pulled up in front of the entrance and frowned. The distaste must have reflected on his face. She caressed his cheek.

"Trust me. It's really exciting. Let's see if the Elvis and Priscilla suite is available. You'll love it."

After checking in as Mr. and Mrs. Jones they entered room sixteen. Justin flipped the switch, and light flooded the room causing him to squint. "What the hell?"

Mirrors were everywhere. Life-size pictures of Elvis and Priscilla were framed with flashing neon lights. A bubbling noise came from across the room. He passed the pink Cadillac bed and noted a Jacuzzi surrounded by mirrors. He stared at the bubbling concoction in the corner. It reminded him of the acid that bubbled just like that in his chemistry class at the university.

"Do you like the room?" He turned around and almost ran into her.

"It's like sleeping with Elvis in the room." All he wanted was a hot shower and a place to lay his tired head. The pink bed didn't appeal to him. "It will do."

She stepped closer and started unbuttoning the top two buttons on his Polo. Her fingers gripped the shirt and pulled it from his jeans, lifting it over his head. She went for his belt and he laid his hand over hers. "What are you doing?"

She glanced up at him and grinned. "I need to dress your wounds and thought we might check out the pink Cadillac and relax before going to the warehouse."

He sat on the edge of the bed and she retrieved the gauze, tape, and antiseptic from the suitcase and knelt in front of him. Once the wound was dressed, he pulled her into his arms. She eased him back on the soft pink comforter and took his nipple into her mouth. Not an experience he had ever had before but he found himself enjoying it. The third leg between his thighs liked it too. She sat up and pulled her shirt over her head. He released the black lace bra and threw it across the room. His hand found her hardened nipple and rubbed it back and forth between his thumb and index finger. She groaned, climbed off of the bed, and stripped out of her jeans.

"You are gorgeous." He reached for her hand and pulled her back on the bed. She leaned over and licked the tip of his cock. He placed his hand on her head as she took him deep in her mouth. She drove him crazy. When he thought it couldn't get any better, she climbed on top and guided him inside of her. It was more than he could take. He pulled back and grabbed her hip. "Wait." He flipped her over on the king size bed. "I want to make love to you. I want to show you what enjoyment can be."

He eased into her and they both went higher and higher until she screamed out his name. It was all he needed to follow her off the edge. He collapsed on top of her. His ribs hurt with every breath. He reached up and touched the side of her cheek and his hand came away wet. She was crying.

He rose off of her. "Are you all right?"

She wrapped her arms around him and pulled him closer. "I'm better than I've ever been."

He eased out of her and pulled her to him. "Tell me about Mara. What was your life like?"

"Why?"

He propped his elbow on the pillow and rested his head in his hand. "Because I want to know everything about you."

She sighed and lay on her back. "It's not a pretty picture."

He kissed her cheek. "I don't care. I want to know you."

"I told you what happened to my mother and father. I guess that started a chain reaction. I lived with various foster parents until one of the family's sons started molesting me. I was ten when it started and I fought him for three years. The school counselor noticed my silence when I entered middle school and I confessed to her. She contacted Social Services and the foster family kicked me out. I went from one home to another. After that I made the decision it wouldn't happen to me again. But I started rebelling and running away. Each time they sent me to another home, I'd run. The last time, no one came looking for me. I always looked older than I was and over developed. I learned fast I could use my body and make a living but I hated doing it. So when one of my customers said I'd make a great stripper, I found The Pink Titty and worked there until Ran offered to take me away with promises of a life of luxury. What a joke. I can't believe I fell for that." She laughed bitterly.

Tears streamed down her face and onto the pillow. He ached for her. His instincts were to comfort and show her she didn't have to live that way. He would erase all those bad memories and replace them with happy ones. "No one deserves what you've been through. I believe I can show you a better life if you'll let me."

She faced him and smiled through her tears. "I'll bet you can."

Two hours later they were on their way to the warehouse. They stopped at a discount store for ground beef and Benadryl. Justin grabbed a roll of paper towels and rubber gloves.

"Ready?" he asked her when their shopping was done.

"Let's do this." She buckled her seat belt.

His hands twitched on the steering wheel as he followed her directions to an industrial area on Cheyenne Avenue. He parked across the street from a tall fence topped with rolled barbed wire. Six eighteen wheelers lined the fence facing the street and a large metal building sat in the back corner of the lot. He was still not comfortable with what they were about to do. Foreboding nagged at him during the cab ride to the rental and on the way to the warehouse. He didn't know if it was because he had never done anything like this before or if they were walking into danger. The fence butted a two-story brick building on the right and he spotted three security cameras mounted on the side, rotating back and forth. This didn't look good.

He opened the door and stepped out. She walked up beside him as he slipped into the gloves "I need to see the dogs so I can estimate their weight. I don't want to hurt them, just make sure they go to sleep."

She handed him the sack, and he unwrapped the hamburger. She put two fingers in her mouth and let out a shrill whistle. Loud barking came from behind the office and it sounded like horses running across the property. The noise would wake any guards they couldn't see. Five Dobermans pounced against the fence letting everyone know of their presence. He estimated the dogs' weight and emptied the correct amount of medicine into the meat. He mixed it together and approached the fence, to the dissatisfaction of the animals. He pitched balls of meat over the fence. At first the animals didn't leave their post, but the smell of fresh beef was too much of a distraction, and they began devouring the treats.

He threw the last ball and walked back to the car. "Now we wait."

"How long will it take?"

He wiped the gloves with the paper towel then stripped them off. "It's hard to say. If their stomachs were empty, it won't take more than fifteen minutes." He leaned against the car. The animals continued searching the ground for additional food.

Twenty minutes later, all five dogs were passed out. "Ready?" He started toward the business.

She grabbed his arm and stopped him. "You wait here. I can work faster alone."

He didn't like the idea of her going by herself but he relented. "Yell if you need me."

"I'll always need you." She kissed him deeply and ran across the street.

***

It didn't take long to pick the lock. She raced to the breaker box that housed the alarm system and disconnected the wires. The red light stopped blinking. Both skills she had learned on the streets. She smiled. She watched the camera movement and dodged the circulation. She rushed across the yard and picked the lock on the metal building and stepped into the dark office. The heavy wooden desk presented a problem. She could have used Justin's help in shoving it away from the trap door underneath. It scraped on the floor when she finally got one corner to move, exposing the door.

She sat on the floor and pulled on the latch. The door slammed backward with a loud clang. She froze. They hadn't spotted anyone but she didn't know for sure. Ran's men could be hiding. After hearing nothing but silence, she took the pen light from her pocket and opened the box Ran had imbedded in the floor. The lid came off with ease. She laid it aside.

In a Ziploc baggy were four flash drives. Under the baggy, she removed a stack of manila envelopes with names written on the front. She pocketed the drives and thumbed through the envelopes. Everyone who lived with or worked for Ran had an envelope. Her name appeared on the last one. Her fingers trembled as she removed the papers and read over them. She gasped. He had dug up dirt on her she had long forgotten. She replaced the papers and folded her envelope and stuck it in the waist of her jeans. She started to return the other envelopes to the box when she spotted another baggy in the bottom. It had one flash drive. Someone had written 'MD' on the bag. She stuck the bag in her shirt pocket and replaced the envelopes. When she went to get up, her foot slipped into the opening in the floor. She fell backwards. Pain shot through her ankle. She used her hands to try and lift her foot from the hole. It wouldn't budge. Wiggling her booted foot sent pain up her leg. She didn't know if it was sprained or broken, but one thing was sure; she had to get out of there.

She sat back and took a deep breath. Panicking wouldn't get her free. Maybe she could slip her foot out of the boot. She reached for the zipper and pulled it down her leg just enough that she could lift her foot out. She sighed. It was easy to get the boot now that her foot wasn't in it. She tried to stand on her left leg, but the ankle wouldn't hold. She bit her bottom lip to keep from crying out. She couldn't hop on one foot, carry her boot, and get back across the yard. When she tried to slip the boot on, her foot had already started swelling. She knew she was working against the clock. The dogs would be stirring soon.

The door opened and she ducked under the desk and held her breath. She put her head to the floor and peeked underneath and saw a man's boots moving across the room. She curled into a ball and hugged her knees. Her heart pounded so loud in her chest, she was sure the intruder could hear it. She tried to breathe as quietly as possible. The desk sat at an odd angle and the lid to the hole lay out in the open.

"Mara. Where are you?"

She released the breath bursting in her lungs. She crawled out from under the desk, welcoming the sight of him. "I hurt my ankle and can't walk."

He wrapped his good arm around her waist and helped her up.

She handed him the single drive. "Hide this one in your boot."

He shoved the jump drive into his boot.

With his help she limped to the door. At the steps, he lifted her like she weighed nothing, carried her down the stairs and started across the lot. The animals were still napping as they approached the fence. They were almost out when lights flooded the yard. They had no place to hide.

"Freeze or I'll shoot."

Bikers came at them from four different directions. From the brick building next to the yard, Ran stepped out of the shadows.

"I'm very disappointed in you, Mara. After all I've done for you and you betray me like this." Something about his calm demeanor scared her more than if he had been screaming.

Her chin shot up. "What are you going to do, Ran? Kill me? You don't have it in you."

The short man grinned. "You might be surprised, my love. No, I won't kill you. I have a better plan. Now your friend here is a different story. He should already be dead but those idiots screwed that up. But that's okay. I'll see to it myself. Rusty, you and Smoker take him to the pens and you take her in the warehouse and tie her up," Ran ordered three gang members. Before she was led away, he grabbed the baggy sticking out of her pocket. He walked back to the limo waiting at the curb and the vehicle pulled away.

Chapter 9

Rusty tied Justin's hands and led him to the Hummer parked at the curb. They were searching him when Cutter shoved her into the warehouse. She hobbled forward and tried to stand on her injured foot but fell.

The biker grabbed her arm and sat her on a chair. He tied her feet to the legs of the chair and her arms behind her back.

"What are you doing, Cutter? You know me. We're friends. You have to let me go."

"It ain't got nothin' to do with that, Mara. I'm doing what the boss said. He'll be back in a little while and I ain't taking the blame if you ain't here. Just sit tight." He disappeared into one of the offices.

She maneuvered her hands up far enough to remove the manila envelope and threw it away from the chair. It landed next to a stack of boxes. *Think, Mara.* Her purse with Justin's cell phone was in the rental. She had no way to contact anyone. Who would she call? Ran had most of Vegas under his thumb. What did he plan to do with her? Kill her and dump her body in the desert? She knew the punishment would be severe. Just like her whole life.

***

Justin strained to see behind him as the leather clad man disappeared into the brick building with Mara. He was rough handled into the back of a Hummer.

"You drive, Rusty." The older guy with a gray beard hanging down the front of his chest climbed in the backseat with him.

Rusty started the car and drove away from the city. Several miles outside of Vegas they pulled down a rutted dirt road that led to a small farm house. After the car stopped, Smoker jerked him from the back seat and shoved him toward a large barn behind the house. A motion-activated flood light came on, loud barking came from inside. Rusty slid the huge door open and the barking increased. The barn was wall to wall crates of dogs. The strong odor of feces and urine penetrated his nose almost knocking him down. His stomach rolled, bile entered his throat. He lowered his head and tried to cover his nose with the material of his shirt.

The older man pushed him into the room causing him to fall on the floor. He closed his hand around sticky dirt and when Smoker lifted him, he slung the grit at the biker's face. The man screamed, rubbed his eyes, and fell into Rusty. They both collapsed backwards. Justin raced to hide in a dark corner behind dog crates. A Rottweiler snapped at the metal bars, trying to reach him. The loud barking prevented him from hearing where the bikers were. The foul odor burned his eyes. He bit his tongue to keep from being sick. He chanced a glance around the crate and saw Smoker hunched over on his knees, still trying to get the dirt out of his eyes. Rusty threw water in the older man's face and Justin heard him snarl in protest.

Rusty glanced in Justin's direction, he ducked behind the crate. "We're gonna cut you up and feed you to the dogs. Do you hear me? You can't get out of here." His voice shook with rage.

"Crap. I can't see." The big guy stood and stumbled over crates, turning in circles and rubbing his eyes. He crashed into one of the few wooden boxes containing a Pit-bull and the crate shattered, landing him on top of the dog. The animal bared his teeth and growled low with his face close to the man.

The man made the mistake of trying to knock the dog away and the animal attacked. The fierce dog drew blood. Justin couldn't watch and turned away.

Bright lights appeared over the interior. A car drove up to the open doors of the barn. Justin dared to look around the crate. The driver got out, left the car running, and opened the back door. Ran stepped out.

"What the hell is going on here?" He demanded.

Rusty straddled the dogs back, trying to pull the animal off of Smoker. The dog wasn't giving an inch, his snapping jaws drawing closer and closer to Smoke's jugular.

"The vet threw dirt in Smoker's eyes and disappeared behind the crates. Don't worry, he's still here."

"For God's sake, help me," Smoker screamed from under the dog.

Justin didn't stick around to see the outcome. He hid deeper behind the hundreds of stacked crates. Several animals had escaped and the men were trying to corral them back into their prisons. He eased one of the doors open, releasing another animal, and went down the line letting dogs loose. They charged toward the criminals, setting off blood curdling screams from the startled men. He crawled toward the door. A broken crate scrapped his leg. He found the sharp metal and sawed back and forth until the ties broke.

"You're toast, Garrett. You can't get out of here without going by us," Smoker yelled.

Loud gunfire echoed in the barn and animals yelped. He knew the fate of some of the dogs, as the rest cowered away from the shots. The open door was only a few feet away when a strong hand pulled him over the top of the crate he was hiding behind.

"Now it's my turn." Smoker dragged him across the dirt and threw him in a chair. Ran picked up a chainsaw and handed it to Rusty.

"Start it. I want to make the first cut and you guys can finish him off."

Rusty yanked on the cord. He hadn't pushed the start button. Until Rusty figured that out, Justin had time to think. He was pretty much out of options, but he had one more card to play. It might not work, but what did he have to lose?

"It won't start," Rusty exclaimed.

Justin held his hands together and looked over his shoulder. Smoker and Ran's driver used cattle prods to keep the dogs at bay. He had to talk fast. "We had a chance to look at spread sheets on the office computer before we left. I bet you guys didn't know your boss is skimming money from your operation. He has a bank account in the Caymans. You're not getting your share. I don't know what your arrangement is, but I bet it's not ninety/ten."

"What's he talking about, Ran?" Smoker lowered the chainsaw.

The older man chewed on his cigar. "Don't listen to him. He's trying to save his skin. Why can't you get that thing started? You're as stupid as the rest of them."

"I want to see those spread sheets. Where are the drives?"

"You can see them when we get back to the house. Now get this job done so we can go." Ran ripped the saw from Rusty's hand and started yanking the cord.

"I want to see 'em now." Smoker grabbed Ran's arm and stopped him. He towered over him.

Ran shoved Smoker away. "I dropped them off at the house before coming here, you idiot."

"I don't believe you. You ain't had time to go back to the house. They're in the car, aren't they?" He started walking toward the running limo. Ran dropped the chainsaw and spun him around, hitting the man on his jaw. The blow had little effect on the large biker. Smoker doubled his fist and knocked the older man into the dirt. The other two bikers dropped the prods and joined the fight. The dogs charged.

Ran covered his face with his hands. Suddenly just a scared little man. The bikers attacked with a vengeance that looked like had been building for a long time.

"Stop! Look, you're getting your share." Ran covered his head with his arms to ward off the fist. "Don't worry about the spreadsheets. You wouldn't know what you're looking at anyway."

Rusty didn't seem to be the brightest star in the galaxy but obviously didn't like being told he was dumb. He kicked at a large pit who had attacked his leg and grabbed Ran by the shirt, lifting the fat man off the ground. "I want to see them."

"They're in the car."

He dropped Ran in the dirt and went to retrieve the drives. He returned with a laptop and the drives, dropped them on the table and opened the computer, booting it up. He plugged the drive into the USB port.

Seemingly forgotten, he waited until the men were huddled around the table, intent on seeing the spreadsheets. In a last ditch effort, he sprinted to the car, jumped in, and shifted into reverse. The tires spun in the gravel as he cut the car into a U-turn and shoved the gearshift into drive. He glanced in the rearview mirror and saw the men running toward the Hummer and peeling out after him. At the main road he took a left and gunned the accelerator. It wouldn't take them long to catch him. He had to get into town and find her.

His heart beat loud in his chest. He looked in the mirror and didn't see the car lights. He whipped into a dark alley next to a couple of boarded up shop fronts and cut the engine. He jumped out, ran to the end of the alley, and hopped the fence, ending up on D Street. A cruiser approached, and he hid in the shadows until it was out of sight. Mara had said she didn't trust the police. He approached the populated area of Vegas and flagged down a cab.

"Desert View Motel."

Heavy traffic slowed the cab to a standstill. He drummed his fingertips on his knee. Twenty minutes later they pulled into the motel. He checked the parking area before going to the room. He shut the door and leaned against it. He flipped the light switch and the Elvis neon above the Jacuzzi blinked its greeting. After checking to make sure the curtains were closed, he switched the neon off and plopped down on the Cadillac bed.

What was he going to do? He was safe for now, but he didn't know how long that would last. What about Mara? Where had they taken her? Could she already be dead? He shook the thought away. He had no experience in rescuing someone. His brothers would know what to do. Should he throw in the towel and make the call? He couldn't go to the cops but what about the FBI? He pulled his shirt over his head and slipped out of his boots. The jump drive fell on the carpet. He picked it up and turned it over and over in his fingers. Those goons didn't even bother to do a thorough search. They were looking for a weapon. In school they used the letters MD to identify the main drive. He had a bargaining tool. He tossed it on the bed and went into the bathroom to wash the stick off.

Chapter 10

Mara tugged on the iron pipe embedded in the concrete. She sneezed in the damp, musty smelling basement. What did he plan to do with her? He could kill her and put her body where no one would ever find it. She didn't think he had it in him. He'd get one of his goons to do the dirty work. Her dilemma worried her but not as much as what Ran intended to do to Justin. They *would* kill him without thinking. They had probably killed him already. Her heart ached. He may have been the only good thing that had ever happened to her and now he was gone. Rage replaced her sorrow. She jerked on the pipe. The zip ties cut into her wrists. She tried kicking herself loose. Nothing worked. She slumped to the floor and laid her head against the cold steel. It was useless.

It didn't matter if she got out of here alive or not if he was dead. Her life without him would be what it had always been, a breeding ground of bad options and worse consequences. The truth was she didn't deserve him. Not after all the things she had done in her life just to survive. Guilt riddled her. She had done this. Ran had forced her to find the doctor and now because of her, he could be dead.

They had taken him to the farmhouse where they kept the dogs. Chills ran over her body. She had been there once and vowed to never go back. The conditions of the animals made her sick. Their blood staining the dirt floor made the interior smell like rotting flesh. If they killed him there, more blood on the floor would go unnoticed. A tear trickled down her cheeks. She moved her face closer to her hand and attached it to her finger. That surprised her. She hadn't cried for someone this much in over fifteen years. He wasn't like anyone she had ever met. He had a kindness that was genuine and an honesty she had never seen before. He treated her with respect. She could be herself around him. Not like an ex-stripper, shacked up with a mobster who had made a deal with one of the worst biker gangs in Las Vegas. That was the life she knew. Perhaps her dream of running away and starting a new life was just that, a dream.

Mara jumped when she heard the door above her creak open and heavy boots coming down the wooden stairs. A light came on that blinded her temporarily.

Dagger approached and Ran walked up beside him. "What am I going to do with you, Mara? I gave you everything. A beautiful home, nice clothes, that motorcycle you wanted so badly. You didn't have to strip or sell yourself or do drugs to forget how shitty your life was. What went wrong? Why would you betray me? Well, this is the last time you will disappoint me. As bad as I hate to see you go, I'm afraid you've been sold."

Her guts tied in knots. She knew what sold meant. Besides selling the fighting dogs, he also ran a trafficking business that supplied prostitutes and sex slaves all over the states. She couldn't believe he was getting rid of her like one of his dogs.

"Where am I going?"

He caressed her cheek. "You'll find out soon enough."

Hate, pure hate for this man ran through her. "Good," she spat out. "It can't be as bad as being your playmate. I'll look forward to leaving."

His evil laugh grated her. "I doubt it. First, I want to know what happened to the main jump drive. Does your boyfriend have it?"

"What are you talking about? You took the bag yourself so I don't have it."

"You know as well as I do that one is missing and I want to know what you did with it."

"Your goons searched me."

He slapped her so hard her head jerked to the side. She tasted a salty metal on her tongue. She glanced at Dagger. Was that a touch of pity she saw in his eyes? She raised her chin and narrowed her eyes in defiance. "I have no idea what you're talking about. Your men must have lost it."

His hand shot up and she raised her head and glared. "You can't beat out of me what I don't have."

He lowered his hand. "Perhaps not. It doesn't matter anyway. I'll find it when I find that boy you're so starry eyed over. You leave in two days for Dubai, United Arab Emirates. I won't ever see you again. I should be sad to lose a piece of ass like you, but there are more junkie whores out there willing to be treated like a lady." He climbed the stairs at the pace of an aging old man. Dagger followed.

Justin was still alive. Excitement overwhelmed her. She wanted to scream with happiness. He must have escaped and they have no idea where to find him. That was the best news she had heard. What was she going to do now? She had to use her charms on someone. But who? She had to get the hell out of this basement and find him before they did. Appealing to Ran was out. How about one of his men? Most of them were so wrapped up in the dog fights and drugs none of them would take her seriously. Except one. Dagger always had a thing for her and she might be able to convince him to help her.

Chapter 11

Justin needed the rental. The keys were still in his pocket, but he wasn't sure if everyone had left the yard where they parked the car. It would mean another trip away from the motel, but the way he saw it he had two choices. The logical one would be to call Rex and ask for help.

"Grow up, Justin." He said aloud.

It might not be logical but he would follow his heart and rescue Mara. If he failed…then chalk another one up to experience. He reached for the room phone. "I need a cab."

"Yes, sir. I'll order one right away."

Taking her back to Texas could put his family in danger unless Ran and his gang were in custody. Until they're captured, he would take her somewhere safe. He had to protect her.

He walked into the bathroom and splashed water on his face. He jumped when the horn blared from outside. After peeking through the curtains, he left the room and got in the cab.

"I need to go to the industrial area on Cheyenne Avenue. I don't know the exact address where I left my car, but I'll recognize the warehouse."

"Tourist," the cabbie grumbled and shot out of the lot. The rental sat in the same spot he had left it.

"There it is." He pointed over the front seat.

The driver pulled up next to the white Camry. "Twenty-one dollars and fifty cents."

Justin handed him his credit card and signed the receipt. The warehouse and yard were empty except for the dogs. They growled through the fence.

He drove toward the motel deep in thought. Where should he start? At the house where it all began? No. Not a good idea. He needed a list to stay focused. A list would keep his objective in place. Locate and rescue Mara.

In the safety of his room, he ate the burger he had picked up at a fast food joint on the way back and made his list. He needed a gun. He didn't dare face that gang without something for protection. Most places wouldn't allow guns and scanned for them but if they cornered him, he would have a weapon. He could pick one up at a pawn shop.

He had to make copies of the jump drive. Finding a place would be easy. He wanted two copies. One to mail home and one to keep with him. If anything happened to him, Rex would open the package he sent. But if he and Mara got away clean, he would lock the copy away as insurance. The other copy he wanted to reference back to if Ran wanted proof.

He needed a physical address and owner of the house where the gang held him. The county records office could supply that and maybe a phone number. He didn't plan to break into the house unless he had to. If Ran cooperated it wouldn't be necessary anyway.

An anonymous call to ASPCA to report the animal abuse was next on the list. By law, it was required by a veterinarian. He could lose his license if they found out he knew and didn't report it. He didn't want to call too early, they might take action, putting Mara's life in danger.

Last on the list was the FBI. He could go to the local bureau now with the drive but it would jeopardize her more. He couldn't risk it. She meant more to him than he dared to admit.

Satisfied and having an action plan in place, he made another list. Across the top of the page he wrote, 'Worst Case Scenario.' He yawned. He hadn't slept in over eighteen hours and his body knew it. Guilt riddled him for resting when she was somewhere possibly fighting for her life. But he knew as a doctor no one, human or animal, ran at top performance deprived of sleep. He couldn't afford mistakes so he forced himself to lay down. Sleep evaded him. He couldn't help but think he had forgotten something. His mind wouldn't give him a break from his problems and after two hours, he went to take a shower. The warm water soothed his sore muscles. After drying off he dressed his wounds as best he could and pulled on a pair of Levis and a blue Polo. He slipped the drive into his boots and put his arm back in the sling. He packed everything he had in the room. After grabbing his list and keys, he left the room. He had to keep moving.

He retrieved his phone from the purse Mara had left in the car and searched for the nearest

Fed-Ex. He keyed in the GPS and found the store within minutes. He walked in and the air conditioner had no effect on the sweat inching down his back. A store employee approached and he jumped when she spoke.

"Do you need any help?"

"I need to make some copies."

She gave him a brief lesson on operation the machine. "When you are finished, I'll bundle the copies for you."

The last page printed and he started to hand the papers to the clerk when he noticed an address at the bottom of the sheet. He smiled and wrote it on a clean sheet of paper.

"I need to send one copy overnight to Texas. The other copy in a separate box."

She took the papers. "I'll get them boxed up for you."

After paying the fee he stuffed the drive back in his boot and took the box. In the car he keyed the address from the paper into the GPS.

He started searching for a pawn shop. It seemed they were on every corner in this neighborhood. He just had to pick one. He passed Gold and Silver Pawn. People were lined up down the sidewalk, waiting to get in. He selected a smaller shop on the next block, parked, and entered the store.

"I'm interested in purchasing a gun. Can you tell me the requirements?"

A big man behind the counter looked him up and down. "If you pass the background check you can pick up your gun in seventy-two hours."

That wouldn't work. He planned to be out of Nevada by then. "Is that the law for the whole state?"

The man shook his head. "Just Clark County."

"Thanks." He left the shop and followed the GPS instructions. Within twenty minutes he passed the massive front gate of the house where he had been held prisoner. The gates were closed and a guard shack sat to the left of the cobblestone driveway. He didn't need in the house; he wanted to know where it was located and who it belonged to for future reference.

He drove down the street and made a U-turn. Now he needed to find the county records office. He keyed in On-Star and asked the disembodied voice for directions. He located the building and parked.

He took an elevator to the third-floor records office. "I need to locate the owner of a house I'm interested in buying." He smiled at the clerk.

An older woman with her graying hair pulled tightly in a bun looked up and smiled. "Certainly. What is the address?"

He retrieved the paper from his pocket and gave it to her. The woman tapped on her computer.

She wrote on a sticky pad and passed him the sheet. "Here you go. That property is owned by Cameron De Luca."

"Does it list a phone number by any chance?"

She glanced at her screen and wrote the number down. After thanking her, he left. Everything was falling into place.

***

Mara's tongue stuck to the roof of her mouth. It had been over eight hours since her capture and she hadn't had anything to eat or drink. Even Dagger hadn't been down to check on her. Did he plan to let her die of thirst? It didn't matter. Her arms ached and her legs tingled all the way to her toes. She would die strapped to a pole in the dingy basement and no one would know. She leaned her head against the cold steel and closed her eyes.

A door slammed and woke her. The visitor's boots echoed through the dark room. Her eyes followed the shadow coming across the room.

"I brought food."

Dagger knelt beside her and caressed her bruised face. This was her chance. She leaned her head into his hand and tried to speak.

"Da…Dagger."

"Here, drink this." He raised a bottled water and she drank the much needed liquid.

"Help me, Dagger! Don't let him do this to me," she pleaded, her tone urgent.

His eyes softened. "He'd kill me, Mara, and you know it. I wish I could. I'll release your hands so you can eat but don't try anything."

He took a switchblade from his pocket and cut the ties. She rubbed her bleeding wrists. "I have to go to the bathroom."

Dagger helped her up. Her legs wobbled and she had to lean on him for support. Her ankle throbbed when she tried to put weight on it. She stepped inside the bathroom and reached to close the door.

"I'll be right here, so don't try anything funny." He pulled the door shut.

She leaned her back against the door. There were no windows, only a sink and toilet. She splashed her face with cold water. The cuts on her wrists burned. She looked around the tiny room for anything she could use as a weapon. Attacking Dagger didn't appeal to her. He could take her down with one hand. But right now, she had no choice, he was the enemy. She lifted the lid from the back of the toilet. The only loose thing in the bathroom. It was heavy. Too heavy for her weak arms. She collapsed on the toilet. She couldn't do it. She didn't have the strength. But this was her only chance.

"Mara, are you done?" Dagger yelled.

"Give me a minute, will ya?"

She lifted the lid with both hands above her head and balanced it. She couldn't hold it and open the door, too. An idea hit her. "Dagger can you help me?"

He opened the door and she swung. His eyes widened, but he had no time to react before the heavy lid slammed into the side of his head. He stumbled backwards and grabbed his head. She dropped the porcelain and bolted for the only way out. Her ankle resisted and slowed her retreat. Her legs were weak, crawling up the stairs was her only option. A hand wrapped around her injured ankle and jerked her back. She screamed in pain. Her arms scrapped against the hard surface. She grabbed for anything she could hold on to as Dagger pulled. Her head bounced like a ball on the unyielding wood.

He lifted her over his shoulder, blood dripping down the side of his face, and carried her back to the pole. He zip tied her wrists once again. "You bitch," he spit out along with a mouthful of blood. He kicked the tray away and stormed up the stairs, leaving her in the dark.

She wouldn't get another chance. She had lived with defeat all of her life. Why should this one be any different?

Chapter 12

Justin drove to a different motel, another disinterested clerk, another room that hadn't seen a vacuum since the eighties. He lowered the temperature and looked up the number for Las Vegas Animal Control. He jotted it down. The law required him to report animal abuse, but if he did before trying to make a deal with Ran, the operation might be moved.

He pulled his cell from his pocket and dialed the number the clerk had given him.

"De Luca residence."

"Mr. De Luca."

"I'm sorry, but Mr. De Luca is not available. May I take a message?"

"Tell him Justin Garrett is in possession of certain documents he is looking for. Let him know I will call back in one hour and don't want to speak to anyone but him." He disconnected.

He checked the time every few minutes. The clock didn't seem to move. He paced. He lowered the air conditioning again but sweat still stained his shirt. He checked the curtains to make sure they were closed and then sat on the bed trying to calm his nerves. He couldn't be rattled when he called back. He had to be in charge.

He looked at his list. He still didn't have a gun and that worried him. What if he got into a situation where he needed one? He might be able to pick one up on the street. That would be taking a chance on the seller knowing Ran. He lowered his head and stared at the floor.

He had half an hour. He grabbed his room key, walked to the main lobby, and stepped up to the counter.

The same clerk that had checked him in sat with his feet propped up on the counter, his eyes glued to a small television. "May I help you?" He didn't look up.

"I need information and I don't know if you can help."

The dark complexion man greeted him with a sleazy smile and put out his hand, palm up. "I'll try."

Justin pulled out his wallet, handed the guy a twenty, and lowered his voice. "I'm going to transport some valuables. I need to buy a gun. Do you have any idea where I can purchase one quick?"

"There's a gun shop on South Highland. Tell 'em Maurice sent ya." The kid shrugged and went back to ignoring Justin.

Justin tried again. "The problem with the gun and pawn shops is they have a seventy-two hour waiting period. I don't have that long."

The young man nodded and leaned across the counter. "I may know someone. I might be willing to help if properly motivated." He held out his hand again. "Of course, street prices ain't cheap. What kind of gun do you want?"

He dug in his wallet again. "I think a Glock with two clips and shells will be fine."

"Be out front in an hour." The clerk pulled out his cell and walked to the back office.

Justin went back to his room and checked the time. Three more minutes. He wiped his hands on his jeans and walked in circles. The clock ticked slowly. At sixty minutes exactly, he dialed the number.

The man who had ordered him killed answered the phone and from the tone of his voice, he wasn't happy. "Boy, where do you get off ordering me around? I'm the one in charge here."

"We'll see about that. I have something you want and you have something I want. I'll make an even trade. No questions asked, no police, and we're both happy."

"How do I know you have it?" Ran growled.

Justin opened the first page and read a small list. "I can go on if you like. There are names, dates, money transfers, and—"

"That's enough. What do you want?"

"Mara. Alive and well."

Ran let out a deep throaty laugh. "What the hell do you want that whore for? She's slept with every man in Vegas. Except for being a fine piece of ass, she's nothing but trouble."

"I'll take my chances. Do we have a deal?" The anxiety inside his chest was eating him up. Ran had to agree. He wanted that drive. He needed it. Would he give her up or was he so angry at her he would refuse and kill her? What if he already had?

"Okay. You've got a deal. But it's on my terms. You meet me at the warehouse and we'll make the exchange."

"No. My terms. We'll meet in the casino of the MGM tonight at eleven at the first dollar slots and don't bring your goons or you'll never see the drive. Just so you know, if anything happens to me or Mara, I've taken precautions. If I disappear, the FBI will be all over your ass. And Ran," he paused, "she had better be with you." He hung up.

***

Ran slammed the receiver down and shook with rage. "That son-of-a-bitch wants to deal with me. With me! He has guts. Gotta give him that. Get the guys together for a meeting," he told Dagger and stormed out of the room.

Ran stomped down the stairs and across the floor until he reached her. The money he was getting for her was sitting in the bank, on hold, pending delivery. If he gave her to the kid, he'd never get it and there would be a lot of angry bikers. He placed his hands on his hips and stared down at her. Her head leaned against the iron pipe. She raised her head and glared at him.

"What do you want, Ran?"

"It seems your boyfriend wants to make a deal. He'll give me the drive if I give him you." She cocked her head to one side. "Do you think that's a fair trade, Mara?"

She straightened her back. "Justin's alive?"

"For now. Are you worth trading?"

"Well considering how much you care about that information and how little you care about me, I think Justin's getting the short end. But if that's what he wants, I say trade."

"You have to go upstairs and get dressed. We're going to the MGM at eleven. Doll up pretty. I love having you on my arm. Cover up those bruises so we'll look good together." He caressed her cheek. She turned her head away.

"Screw you. Get away from me. I'm not going anywhere with you."

He didn't like her answer and swung at her, catching her on the mouth. "Now look what you made me do." He took her chin in his hand and glared at her. "You will go, you will be devoted to me, and you will deny that you want to leave with him. If you don't, I will kill you both before you get four blocks from the Grand."

He walked to the bottom of the stairs. "Dagger will be down to get you in a few minutes. Don't try anything or I'll have him shoot you on the spot. Just remember where you are and what I have you here for."

He ascended the steps and headed toward his sitting room. His hands doubled into fists. This country hick wasn't about to upstage him. He already had a plan.

He walked in the room full of bikers and went to the liquor cabinet, poured a straight shot of scotch, gulped it down, and poured another. He held the glass and stared at the scruffy beards and yellow teeth sitting around the room. "I want four of you at the MGM Grand within thirty minutes. Each will take a different position in the casino. Stay in the background, but close enough to take this Texan down and get that stupid drive. Two of you stay here and the rest of you set up along Tropicana. He knows too much to get away. I'll be there with Mara at eleven but I don't intend to make an exchange. She's going to the Sheik tomorrow night if I have to take her myself. Any questions?"

The men left and he sipped his drink, lit one of his Cuban cigars, and sat in a chair next to the fireplace. There was only two things the vet could have done as precautions. Make a copy or emailed the drive to someone. That bothered Ran. If the spreadsheets fell into the wrong hands, he would be ruined.

***

Justin stood in the shadows of his motel thirty minutes later. He had used both his debt and credit cards at the ATM in the office to withdraw the amount he might need. A few minutes later a dark blue Corvette pulled up, the door flew open.

"Get in." The driver wore a baseball cap pulled low over his eyes, wraparound sunglasses, and had a well-trimmed beard. "Hurry up, dude."

Justin slid into the seat. The driver pulled out of the motel, driving to a discount store before parking a good distance from the store.

He didn't know if the chill bumps on his arms were from the cold air blasting from the air conditioner or the fact he had just climbed in the car of a stranger. He wiped his damp palms on his jeans. "Did you bring it?"

The guy stared at him for a few seconds. "Are you a cop?"

The question took him aback. "No."

"I need to see an ID."

He pulled his wallet out and went to retrieve his driver's license. The man ripped the wallet from his hands. He looked at the driver' license then took all the money. He threw the wallet in Justin's lap and counted the bills.

"Hey! What are you doing?" He picked up the empty wallet.

The man reached for the black case in the back seat and set it on the console, flipping the lock. "My prices vary. If you could get one at the gun shop, we wouldn't be sitting here, would we? I don't have all night. Do you want it or not?"

Justin picked up the Glock from the foam padding and checked the chamber. He found two clips in the case plus several rounds of ammo. "I'll take it." He placed it back in the case, shut the lid, and reached for the door handle.

"Hold on. I'll take you back. Free of charge."

In his room he pitched the gun on the bed and filled both clips. He then inserted one clip in the gun and put the other in his pocket. He closed the case and shoved it under the bed. He checked the sighting down the barrel. After securing the safety he stuck the gun in his boot. He grabbed his keys, stuffed the copy of the drive into a bag and made sure he had the bargaining item in the other boot. He hoped Ran would believe he had all copies plus the drive and would trade without objection.

In the car he laid his head on the steering wheel. This just had to work. He drove out of the parking lot and headed for the meeting at the Grand.

Chapter 13

Perspiration ran down Justin's spine. He had to get to the casino before Ran and his men. The traffic had eased up and he made the drive in record time. Handing over the keys to a valet, he entered the hotel. He scanned the river of people but didn't see a familiar face. Gamblers were shoulder to shoulder and every slot machine occupied. Others stood around waiting for players to abandon their seat. He ventured into the chaos and headed to a bar close to the front door.

He found a seat with a clear view of the entrance and ordered a soda. His hand shook so hard when he picked up the drink, it spilled on the bar. He needed something stronger but couldn't chance it. If this didn't work, the only option left was to contact Rex and the authorities.

He concentrated on keeping an eye on the front door. A woman sitting two stools away interrupted. "Are you waiting for someone?"

He glanced over and she scooted next to him. "Yes. She'll be here soon." He swiveled on his stool and saw Mara entering the casino holding on to Ran's arm. "There she is now. Excuse me."

The woman looked toward the door, gasped, and grabbed his arm. "I hope you aren't waiting for Mara. She's Raniero's property and it looks like they're here together."

He swallowed the rest of his soda and stood. "She won't be for long." He walked out of the bar.

Mara wore a pair of large sunglasses. A bruise darkened her left cheek. His hands squeezed into fists. He'd kill Ran for hurting her. He wove through the crowd and stood in front of them. She smiled at him and moved closer to Raniero. The hair on the back of his neck stood on end. Something was wrong.

The older man patted her hand where it rested on his arm and he glared at Justin. "I believe you have something for me."

He studied her face. He couldn't see her eyes behind the dark glasses. "Give it to him, Justin. Ran and I have worked out our differences and I'll be staying."

He clenched his teeth together. What the hell was she doing? "I don't—"

"Are you Justin Garrett?"

Four police officers surrounded him. "I am," he said slowly.

"Mr. Garrett, we have a warrant for your arrest," one of the officers informed him.

Justin frowned. "For what?"

The cop took his arm. "Attempting to extort money from Mr. De Luca. You need to come with us."

He looked at Ran and fumed at the wide grin on his face. "What about him?" He pointed. "He's abducted this woman and is holding her against her will."

The officer looked at her. "Is that true, Ma'am?"

She tighten her hold on Ran's arm. "No. That's not true. I don't have any idea what he's talking about."

"Don't give us any trouble, Mr. Garrett." The officer pulled him toward the exit.

"Wait." Ran stopped them. He jerked the bag out of Justin's hand and searched inside. "This isn't all. He still has the drive. Search him."

Justin narrowed his eyes and growled through gritted teeth. "This isn't over."

Ran chuckled. "I think it is."

The cops led him to a small room the casino designated and ordered him to remove his clothes. He had made the right decision to make an extra copy. Once Ran had the drive, he would believe he had all the evidence.

Chapter 14

Mara wiped the tear that slid down her cheek. That had been the hardest thing she had ever done. She stared at the bright lights of the city she had known for most of her life. The car drove out of town. She could have told the truth at the hotel but as long as Justin was arrested in the casino with all those witnesses, they wouldn't harm him. If she had said Ran was holding her against her will, he would have been released and dead shortly thereafter. She couldn't take that chance with his life. At least at the precinct he could contact his brother.

"You're awfully quiet, Mara. Aren't you going to try to talk me out of shipping you out?"

She sighed and continued to stare out the window. "Would it do any good?"

His laugh grated on her. Her hand clenched the door handle and she fought the urge to slap the shit out of him. There had to be a way out of this. She just had to think.

They pulled through the massive gate and up to the front of the house. Dagger opened the car door and pulled her out. She stumbled in her heels and he held her arm to keep her from falling. She moved closer to him and whispered so Ran wouldn't hear. "Please, Dagger. If you help me out of this we can run away together. Just you and me. He'll never find us."

His eyes narrowed and his lips pressed tight together. She couldn't tell if there would be help from him or not. Dagger had saved her from Ran's temper more than once. Why not now?

He pulled her into the house and started toward the basement. She jerked her arm out of his grip. "No. I will not be put back in that dungeon. I'm going to my room and you can lock me in. I'm sleeping in my bed."

Ran grabbed her arm and turned her around. "You forget who this house belongs to. I will let you spend your last night in the room you have been using. Dagger will be posted outside and the door locked. Enjoy. It will be the last

pleasant night you have for a very long time."
He disappeared into the library.

Dagger took her arm again and led her
upstairs. "C'mon Buttercup. I guess you won
this one."

She cringed at the nickname he had given
her when she first came to the house. He was
the only person who called her Buttercup and
never said it so anyone else could hear.

After she heard the lock click, she checked
the room for bugs and cameras but didn't find
any. That had been the first thing she and Ran
had a difference of opinion on. She wanted her
room free of any electronics. Taking one more
look around and satisfied the room was clear,
she pulled a chair into the closet. From behind a
stack of shoe boxes on the top shelf she pulled
the black leather tote.

One of the things she had learned when she
had been shipped from foster family to foster
family was always have her crap packed and
ready to go. As an adult this lesson had become
even more ingrained when she had been
escaping abusive boyfriends or landlords she
didn't have the money to pay. She kept a crash
bag always ready to go. She dumped the

contents on her bed. A burner phone, charged, a couple of thousand in cash, a few pieces of jewelry that could be pawned, a change of clothes and a make-up kit. She picked up the phone and opened the web app containing her computer. Did Justin tell her his brother's name? She keyed in Garrett Quarter Horse Ranch in Texas. A beautiful picture of a herd of horses popped on the screen. The names Carson and Rex Garrett came up. She hit the contact link.

To FBI Agent Rex Garrett. Your brother, Justin, is in jail for extortion. He is in extreme danger. He was supposed to mail important documents to Texas that will prove his innocence. Contact the Las Vegas FBI and get him into protective custody immediately before he is killed.

She hit the send button, repacked the bag including the burner, stowing it back in the depths of her closet and went to take a shower. All she could do now was wait and hope. She glanced in the mirror over the sink and was shocked at how dark the bruise marks had gotten. She could cover them with makeup but it made her feel better to flaunt them in front of Ran. She doubted he felt any kind of remorse but maybe one of the others would feel sorry for her.

Stripping out of her Gucci gown, she let it drop to the floor like a rag and stepped into the glass shower. The warm water made her feel better. When she finished, she dried off, slipped into a long silk rose-colored gown and crawled under the down comforter. Her stomach growled.

She threw the cover back and picked up the phone. She punched in the kitchen and Dora answered. "I'm hungry, Dora. I haven't eaten since yesterday. Is there anything you can fix me?"

"*Si.* You want chicken salad with crackers or on a sandwich?"

"Sandwich will be fine. Do you have any cheesecake?"

Dora chuckled. "You know I keep cheesecake for you, Ms. Mara. I will bring it to you right away." The cook hung up.

She was clean, had clean clothes, and would have her belly full. No way to know when she would get to eat again. She was going to enjoy it while she could.

Chapter 15

Misty stepped into Rex's office. "I have a message on my computer you need to read."

"Can't you take care of it? I'm in the middle of the Copeland case and it's taking up all of my time."

Misty walked over to his desk and leaned her palms on top. "It's on the ranch account and it's about Justin. He may be in trouble. I'll send it to your computer, hold on."

Rex read the message. The muscles in his back tightened. An icy chill seeped into his veins. "Get the Las Vegas FBI on the phone and transfer them to me," he called out to Misty.

He ran his shaky hands through his hair. This is why they hadn't been able to get in touch with him. He hadn't answered his phone, had left the hotel, and they didn't know where he went. Rex hadn't been concerned until now. He thought his brother was blowing off some Vegas steam, met a girl, and they were taking in some of the shows.

"They're on line three," Misty yelled through the open door.

Once he had the agent on the line, he tried to make his tone more worried than accusing. After all, there might be a chance this was someone's idea of a cruel joke. "This is Agent Rex Garrett in Tyler, Texas. I've received information that my brother, Justin Garrett, may have been arrested and is being held by the LVPD. The information I got implied that he could be harmed while in custody. Can you verify that he is in jail and call me back?"

Agent Knolls assured him they would let him know something within the hour. Rex went to pour himself a cup of coffee. On his way back to his office he stopped at Misty's desk. "Do we ever have fresh coffee?"

She laughed. "We do at eight in the morning and no one drinks the whole pot. It sits there and makes sauce. Do you want me to make a fresh pot?" She was already up and headed to the break room.

"Don't worry about it." He kept moving toward his office. It was too early to call Carson and he sure didn't want his mom to know anything until he had more details. Please let this be a prank, he prayed.

He checked his watch every five minutes. An hour and a half later, he was about to call Las Vegas back when the phone startled him. "Garrett."

"Agent Garrett this is Agent Knolls in Las Vegas. You brother has been arrested for extortion due to a complaint by Mr. De Luca. That's all I know at the moment. Do you want us to put him in lock-up here at headquarters?"

"Yes, I do. I'll be on a plane this afternoon. I should be in Las Vegas about five hours after that. I'll contact you when I arrive."

"No problem. What do we list as the official reason we are taking him into custody?"

"He's a material witness in an out-of-state murder trial, should do it."

Chapter 16

They brought food that he didn't have the stomach to eat so he gave it to a man in dirty clothes and a scraggly beard. The man was tall and skinny with long hair that hadn't seen a comb in weeks.

"Thank you, man."

Justin rested his head in the palms of his hands and propped his elbows on his knees. Why would she deceive him? How could she be such a fake? The excitement and bright lights of Vegas might appeal to her more than a country home with horses. The high rollers, casinos, and country clubs had been her life. She fit in here, not Texas. If this life was what she wanted then she could have it. But why would she stick around for abuse and humiliation at Ran's hands? Why didn't she run away? She had run before. He had to be coercing her with something she cared more about than herself. But what?

"Justin Garrett."

He stood at the bars. "That's me."

The guard unlocked the door. "You're being moved. The FBI is here to take you downtown to their lockup."

Why would the fed's be moving him? This didn't make sense. He walked out of the cell and followed the officer through the narrow hall. They stepped up to a counter in the small outtake area. The man behind the counter poured out the contents of an envelope. "Is this everything you came in with?"

He counted his money, checked his cards and driver's license, keys, and a handful of change. They had kept the gun found in his boot. "I believe it is."

"Sign here." The officer took the signed sheet. "He's all yours, fellows."

Two men in dark suits stepped up to him. "I'm Special Agent Knolls and this is Agent Patterson. We are taking you to another facility until you are arraigned."

He hadn't seen any identification. Justin's heart rate went up. Were they actually agents or corrupt cops? This could be his end.

"Why is the FBI picking me up?" No one answered. "Can I see some ID?" One of the agents, he wasn't sure which was which, took his arm and guided him outside and into a black SUV. They drove up the strip and left the busy part of Las Vegas.

The driver opened his wallet and showed Justin identification and badge that looked like his brothers. Justin stared out the window unable to comprehend what was happening. His curiosity ate at him until he couldn't stand it any longer. "Can someone tell me what's going on?"

"We received orders to pick you up from LVPD. Seems you may have happened on something you shouldn't have, son. This may be the same organization we've been investigating for three years. They've kept right under the radar and we haven't been able to get anything on them. It might help if you tell us what you know."

So the agents were legit. "I don't know a lot." The agent looked in the rearview mirror at him skeptically. "I don't! Mara is the one you want."

"And who is Mara?"

"She's…well, she's a woman who lives with Raniero De Luca. She kept the records at the waste disposal business for a while. But she knows all about his other activities, too. I'm sure she's at his place outside the city. I thought she was leaving him but…" He waved his hand.

"You don't think so now?"

"No. I think he's forcing her to stay with him. We planned to leave together. She wanted away for Vegas."

"She might have changed her mind. Besides, De Luca is a pretty big fish here in Las Vegas. Word is he married into the Sicilian mob and they set him up here. He runs drugs mostly. Although he partnered up with one of the most vicious gangs last year and they've been up to no good. He's been doing his best to get into sex trafficking. He's a slippery character and has people everywhere."

"Don't forget about the dog fights," Justin said.

Knolls turned sharply in the seat. "What dog fights?"

He told them about the animal abuse at the house and how he had been brought to save Ran's prize dog. "Mara didn't know they planned to kill me whether the dog lived or died."

"We had no idea. We'll notify animal control. I'll call them as soon as you fill us in. I want to hear about the girl. Is she in on the action?" Knolls looked over the seat at him.

She might have been at one time but not the Mara he knew now. She didn't belong here. She had grown up hard, no one would deny that but to be an active part in sex trafficking? Drug running? No.

"I don't think so," he finally said.

Agent Patterson stopped at a red light. Loud rumbles startled Justin. To the right a dozen or so bikers made a left and the back window of the SUV shattered. Glass splattered over the seat, barely missing him.

"Get down, Justin. Step on it." Knolls keyed the radio. "Shots fired. Corner of Bell and

Martin Luther King." The SUV took a sharp right, squealing tires.

He unbuckled his seatbelt and flopped down on top of the glass shards. His heart jumped into his throat, cutting off his air. The rumble faded when sirens approached.

The car made several more sharp turns before pulling up in front of a squat, nondescript building on the outskirts of town. Knolls opened the back door and rushed him inside to the elevators. The bell dinged and the doors opened on number four. The agents stuck their heads out, checking the hall before escorting him to a set of rooms as plain as the façade of the building.

The two agents walked into the room, went around the living and dining area to the window, and checked the street outside. Satisfied they hadn't been followed, Knolls shed his jacket.

Justin walked over to the window and stared out at the retreating sun. The darkness brought glowing lights of Las Vegas, not dimmed at all even though he knew they were quite a distance from the strip. His insides quivered and his heart pounded. How the hell had he gotten mixed up in anything so dangerous? He was a vet for God's sake!

"Away from the window," Patterson ordered gruffly. His phone buzzed. "Patterson. Okay. Thanks. That was Agent Byers. They didn't find the bikers. There will be patrols the rest of the night."

"I need a drink." He stepped over to the kitchenette. Looking around the dismal apartment he guessed he wouldn't find any liquor. He settled for a glass of water. His hand trembled as he lifted the glass. The cool liquid soothed the tight muscles in his throat. He plopped into a chair next to the couch.

"Why did the FBI take me out of the lockup?"

Patterson sat on the sofa, loosened his tie, and leaned back. "Your brother called us."

His eyes widened. "Rex?"

"Yeah. He asked us to get you into protective custody."

He tried to wrap his head around how Rex could have gotten involved in his mess. "How did he know I was in jail?"

Knolls took a seat next to Patterson on the couch and shrugged. "Have no idea."

Patterson sat forward and rested his elbows on his knees. "What can you tell us about the Warlords and De Luca?"

He ran his hand across his face. "The Warlords are mean as hell and take orders from Ran. Anything he says, goes." He proceeded to tell them everything he had personally witnessed or heard. He kept Mara's involvement to a minimum other than to say she had been Ran's mistress for the last two years.

"Do you know where the farmhouse is?"

He nodded. "I think so. They didn't blindfold me on the way to the house. I guess because they planned to feed me to those poor animals. It's about ten minutes west of Vegas."

Chapter 17

Justin refilled his water glass. "I need to get my stuff from the Sunset Motor Court. It's a hole on Fremont. I want to get a shower, put on some clean clothes, and I need to change these bandages."

"If you have a key, I'll send someone over to pick them up." Patterson stood.

An hour later, he had finished his shower, changed his bandages, and gotten dressed. The wounds were looking a bit less angry. He went back into the sitting area where the two agents waited. "How long are we going to be here?"

"We're going to raid the farmhouse. As soon as backup arrives, we'll get you to show us where to go. We've contacted animal control and the local SPCA. They're waiting on our call to roll."

His stomach churned at the thought of all the caged animals. With dogs trained to fight it would be a long road to rehabilitate them into pets someone would feel safe enough to have in their home. Each dog would have to be evaluated physical and mentally before any decision would be made about their fate. He prayed that most of the dogs were redeemable and none had to be put down. Abuse of any innocent human or animal made him sick. If he could, he would take them all. "I'm ready when you are."

Patterson's phone buzzed. "Everyone's ready."

Justin and Knoll waited in the lobby while Patterson checked the area then pulled a new SUV close to the building entrance. He scooted into the backseat. They picked up four more vehicles at the edge of town along with several vans from animal control. He instructed Patterson to take highway eighty west.

Justin checked all the side roads they passed until he spotted the right one. "Turn right on this county road. It's about three miles to the driveway."

Patterson eased into the drive and turned off the lights. The agent slowed and followed the road until the farmhouse came into view. He hit the blue and red lights on the SUV and pulled in front of the barn. The double doors were bolted with a chain and padlock. An agent who he hadn't seen before popped his trunk and retrieved bolt cutters. Barking from the animals inside filled the night.

"You sit right here. This is a raid and I don't want you hurt," Patterson ordered before the agents exited the vehicle, leaving him alone.

He couldn't sit and do nothing. Thirty seconds after the order, he stepped out of the car. He became lost in the crowd of people with nets, tranquilizer guns, and metal animal carriers.

The doors were slid open and the growls and barking increased. The inside flooded with light. Justin grabbed the arm of a woman wearing a khaki uniform. "Is there a medical bag? I'm a vet." She shoved a box into his hands then disappeared inside the barn.

He went to work checking the crates for any animals with cuts or injuries that wouldn't make it to a clinic. He found a dark pit who wasn't barking. He reached for the door to open the cage and the dog growled. Checking the bag, he found the medicine and syringe needed to calm the dog. He filled the syringe and gave the shot.

"Easy boy. I'm not the enemy," he said in a calm voice after sedating him. The dog whimpered as he fell asleep. "There you go." He eased the door open and slid the animal out of the crate and ran his hands over the body. "You have a bad leg. Let's get that taken care of first."

Once he had wrapped the leg and stitched a bad cut, he carried the sleeping pit to one of the vans and turned him over to an animal control officer. "I set his leg and sewed up a cut. He'll be fine."

The rep took the pit and eased him into a padded crate. "Would you take a look at another one in the other van? I don't think he's going to make it."

He spent the next two hours administering medical assistance to injured animals. He worked tirelessly and only lost one dog. Tears clouded his vision.

A hand patted him on his back. "It wasn't your fault, Doc. He was almost gone before we got here. I'm glad you didn't stay in the car. Mad about it, but glad." A pinched smile brushed Patterson's mouth.

If he could get his hands on Raniero right now, he would gladly go to jail for assaulting that piece of vermin. By the time they had all the dogs loaded, he was ready to collapse. He was tired but the rage surging through him kept his adrenaline pumping. He clenched his jaw so hard his teeth hurt.

"It's strange that there were no guards," Patterson said on the way back to town. "They were tipped off."

Patterson looked at Justin in the back seat. "Only one person got bit. Everyone used extraordinary caution. Could have been a lot worse."

"That animal will be quarantined until they're sure there's no rabies," he told him.

"What happens if it turns up he has it?"

He ran his hand across his face. "They'll put the dog down. The person will have to start a series of rabies shots. It's a long and painful process."

Patterson pulled into the parking lot of the apartment building. "Let's try to get some sleep. Tomorrow will be a busy day. We'll have Judge Williams issue a search warrant for the house."

Once inside the apartment, Justin went to the fridge for a much needed drink. He carried the soda into the bedroom and stripped. After adjusting the water in the shower, he stepped in. Streams of blood mixed with water washed down the drain.

He wanted to get the image of the warehouse out of his head. Several of the animals might not survive and his heart broke for them. He would offer his services to the one of the clinics that housed the rescued dogs. He leaned his head against the tile. Right now, he needed sleep.

Chapter 18

After a restless night, Mara rose early. She pulled her bag from the closet and found the number for the LVPD and dialed.

"Las Vegas Police Department."

"This is Mr. De Luca's assistant and he wants to know the status of Justin Garrett. You arrested him last night. Mr. De Luca wants to know if anyone posted his bail."

She heard the clicking of a computer keyboard. "He has been released into the custody of the FBI."

"Thank you. I'll let him know." She clicked the phone off and threw her arms in the air. "Yes." He was out of Ran's reach. She could now defy him without worrying about Justin's fate.

She gathered her clothes and went to take a shower. With her grooming complete, she entered the bedroom and jumped when she saw Ran sitting on her bed.

"The farm was raided and they took the dogs. Your boyfriend was there with the FBI and those pain-in-the-ass animal people. I don't suppose you know anything about this."

After she composed herself she opened the door to her walk-in closet and pitched her gown in the hamper. "You know where I've been for the last twenty-four hours. How the hell am I supposed to know about any raid?"

He rose and stood in the doorway, blocking her exit from the closet. "The guys and I think they'll raid the house next. So we need to get out of here. The plans have changed. Your plane leaves tomorrow. You won't need clothes." He walked to the bedroom door. "Dagger will be up to get you in a few minutes."

He closed the door and she heard the lock. She leaned her head against the closet frame. She didn't want to cry. She had no way out. At least Justin was out of danger. His brother would make sure he got home safely. This was her life. A sad existence. You either used or were used. Nothing ever lasted except pain and misery. No one was coming to save her. Hell, no one would even miss her. She wiped the tears from her cheeks. There had never been anyone she cared enough about to rescue and try to protect. Until Justin. As long as he was okay, she could endure what life had in store for her. She dressed and sat on the foot of the bed to await her fate.

Dagger stepped inside. "Let's go."

She stared at him. "Where are we going?"

"What does it matter to you?"

She had heard Ran talk about a safe house he had tucked away, but she had never been there and had no idea where it was. She wished they hadn't taken her cellphone. She didn't dare bring the hidden bag. They'd only confiscate it. She could have contacted the FBI and let them track her phone. "Do you know where or not, Dagger?"

He shrugged. "Only he knows. He thinks there's a rat in the group so he's pretty tight lipped. Guess we'll know when we get there. Move it."

Ran leaned against a Range Rover with his arms crossed over his chest when they reached the outside. It seemed like she was running but when Dagger shoved her forward, she realized she had been dragging her feet.

They drove out the gate and turned away from Vegas. Dagger followed on his black Harley.

***

Justin awoke to the sound of voices. One sounded familiar. He threw the comforter back and opened the door into the sitting room. Rex rose from his chair.

He rubbed his eyes with his palm. "What are you doing here?"

Rex walked over and hugged him. "Nice to see you, too."

"When did you get in?"

Rex returned to the loveseat. Justin took a chair across from him. "Late last night. You were asleep. When I heard you were in trouble, I had to come. By the way, I received your package." He narrowed his eyes. "That's some powerful stuff. That was good thinking, bro."

Justin sat and propped one leg over the other. "I had good teachers. Seriously, how'd you find out I was in jail?"

Rex poured coffee from the Styrofoam container on the table. "It's really strange, actually. An email came in on the ranch website. No signature; just a note telling me you were in the hands of people who intended to harm you. I contacted these guys." He waved his hand at Patterson and Knoll. "They had no problem transferring you out."

Patterson sat forward on his chair. "A warrant has been issued this morning for De Luca, members of the Warlords, and some of the LVPD based on the evidence you sent to your brother. It's bigger than we thought. De Luca has disappeared. When the agents went to the house to arrest them, the place was empty. We've got forensics, DEA, and FBI all over it."

Justin rubbed the back of his neck. "Mara's with him."

"She may already be dead. He may have decided she was the snitch and had his goons kill her. I'm sorry to say it, but you need to be prepared for that possibility. These are hard, desperate people. They're going to make some very bad decisions before this is over." Patterson looked at Rex. "You were right about the cops being on his payroll, by the way. An FBI agent, too. That's who fired that shot yesterday. None of them are talking though. I don't think any of them knew the extent of the operation and didn't want to as long as they were receiving an envelope with cash in it every month. They feed Ran and the gang information and the money to them flowed."

For a while, Justin listened to the three agents discuss the evidence and their next move. He had to do something. He couldn't just sit here dwelling on the loss of Mara. If he knew where to go, he would confront her. But at this point he had nowhere to look. It might have been best in the long run. Taking her home could have put the rest of his family in danger.

The shop talk was driving him crazy. He rose and went into the bedroom to dress. He was going to do something useful that would keep him from thinking about her.

He entered the small living room and interrupted the agents. "I'm going to the clinic where most of the badly injured animals were taken and see if I can help with the dogs picked up last night."

Rex stood. "The only place you're going is Texas."

Justin's blood boiled. His nerves were at the tips of his fingers and he didn't like being told what he could and couldn't do anymore. It was time he stood up to his older brothers. He glared at him. "I'm not trained to fight crime but I *am* trained to help those animals that were rescued. I know for a fact they are short on doctors and need the extra help. I'm going to the clinic to do what I can. That's what I'm trained to do."

"What if De Luca comes after you again?" Rex argued.

He pointed at Patterson. "He just said De Luca has disappeared. He won't take a chance on being caught coming after me. I'm going. I don't need your permission." His insides burned. He didn't like standing up his brother, but it was long overdue. He was a grown man and his brothers still treated him like a baby. No more. He had completed his education, had one-fourth of a thriving business, and he could take care of himself. He had grown up.

***

The Range Rover wound through the mountains and pulled into a concrete drive with an iron gate. Ran rolled the window down and keyed in numbers. The gate opened. He parked in front of a small ranch style house. If circumstances had been different, she would have enjoyed exploring the house and surrounding woods.

She stepped out and looked around. It was a lovely older home with a gazebo covered in dead vines. The paint trim on the house had started to peel. She followed Ran up the steps. A bird squawked and flew out from under the covered porch.

"Eeek." She rushed inside the house and stared out the door.

He laughed. "Don't worry. You'll only be here a short time before you have to catch a plane."

Dust covers draped the furniture and a layer of film covered the windows. The house hadn't been used in a while.

"Dagger will put the groceries in the kitchen. I sent him shopping earlier so we would have food. You get to cook." He walked away leaving her to stare after him.

She knew how to cook but had only been in the kitchen when most of the house slept. Besides, a few groceries didn't stock a kitchen. She followed Dagger down the hall. He sat several brown paper bags on the island in the center of the room. Before she could prepare something to eat, she had to eliminate the dirt.

She spent the next half hour clearing away the layers of dust on the dishes. After preparing a platter of sandwiches, she grabbed one and stepped out on the back deck. The wind whistling through the trees made a mournful sound as if mocking her mood.

Where was he now? Probably back in Texas. She had never been to Texas. As a matter of fact, she had never been out of Nevada. Born into a dysfunctional family, her life had followed the same path ever since. Living on the street had taught her to become tough to survive. She got mixed up with the wrong people and started using in order to get through the johns and perverts. Thank God, Dixie helped her get clean and off the streets. Now, she didn't know where he was sending her. It couldn't be as bad as turning tricks.

Chapter 19

Justin pulled a card from his wallet and gave the address to the cabbie he flagged down.

The car pulled up to the front door of Siena Animal Hospital on South Grand Canyon. He entered and walked up to the reception desk.

"I'm Justin Garrett, DVM. I was at the raid last night and I've come to offer my assistance with the animals that were brought in."

The young girl pushed a buzzer and rose. "We're happy to have you. Come this way and I'll get you a white coat."

Once he had the coat on, she led him past several examining rooms. They stepped into a large warehouse filled with pet carriers lining the walls. Stainless tables had been set up in the middle and several men and women stood at each table examining or doing minor surgery on sleeping dogs.

"Doctor Tam, this is Doctor Garrett. He was at the raid last night and is here to help," the receptionist introduced him.

"I'd shake your hand, Doctor, but mine are a little tied up at the moment. I'm very glad you're here. We're taking the most injured first and working our way through. We sorted them and they're against the wall. Start from the left and work your way down the line. The girls will get any supplies you need. Just pull another table over and grab a dog. Be careful until they're sedated." He addressed one of his assistants. "Bev, you can help Doctor Garrett. I think Jennifer and I can handle this."

Justin nodded. "Thanks. Let me know if you want me anywhere else. I'm trained in surgery if you find the need." He pulled a table away from the wall. He told Bev what he needed from the supply room and she disappeared. Justin went over to the next crate in line. A black and white pit bull growled.

He reached for the dog treats his assistant had handed him and waved it in front of the cage. "Now listen, buddy. I'm here to help you and if you bite me then I can't. So let's get off to a good start by having breakfast together." He handed the animal the treat and the pit inhaled it in one bite. The young assistant returned, handed him a bottle of Telazol, he loaded a syringe and opened the cage. The animal growled but didn't attack. With the aide's help he was able to administer the shot. Pain shot up his broken arm when he pulled it out of the sling. It didn't matter, he needed both hands. He would endure. Whatever discomfort he was going through, these animals had been through a hundred times worse.

"Good boy. Are you ready for me to take a look at you?" He reached down and slowly picked up the dog and set him on the table.

For the next several hours he worked on the animals. He had finished with a brown pit and started for the next animal when another doctor stopped him. Doctor Baker was written on his blood-stained white jacket. "Time for a break, doctor. You've been at this none-stop. Come with me and I'll show you where you can wash up and then we'll get a bite to eat."

Justin glanced at his watch. It was after three. Where did time go? He followed the older doctor to a surgical wash room. After cleaning up, they went into the break room. Several trays of sandwiches sat in the middle of a table.

"What would you like to drink?"

Justin pulled out one of the chairs and collapsed. "Anything will be fine."

The doctor set a Coke down and pulled out a chair across from him. "You'll need the caffeine." Doctor Baker filled his plate. "You're an excellent doctor, Garrett. I could use someone like you."

Justin grabbed a paper plate and picked up two sandwiches. "I appreciate the compliment, but I have a job." He bit into the chicken salad and his stomach growled. He hadn't eaten today and his body was letting him know. "Does the clinic assist in a lot of rescues?"

Doctor Baker took a sip of Coke and stared at his can. "Yes. We are the largest clinic in Vegas and any time there is a number of rescues, animal control calls us. This is the worst one I've seen."

"How often do you get confiscated animals?"

"Last year we averaged four times. This year started off fast. It's only March and we've had two."

Justin lost his appetite and shoved the plate away. "Do you place them all or do some have to be euthanized?"

Dr. Baker set his food down and looked across the table. "The animals are kept for two years. They are trained, walked, and socialized with other people and animals. There have been some that just couldn't be re-trained. Those had to be put down. But those are too few to count. We have an excellent record for adoptions.

Chapter 20

Lost in her musing, Mara jumped when the door behind her opened. Ran stepped out onto the patio and sat next to her.

After a long silence, he asked, "What makes him different from all the others?"

She knew who he was talking about but didn't answer.

He leaned back in the chair. "You've never been attracted to anyone and there have been a number of men who would pay for a chance with you. Why him?"

"Most of the men I've been with never treated me with respect. I know who and what I was, Ran. No one took the time to see the real person buried deep inside hidden underneath the bad stuff. Believe it or not, I have values and in the short time I was with him, he treated me the way I want to be treated. He didn't judge me."

He stood and shoved the chair back. "Once a slut, always a slut, is what I say. I hope you're happy half way across the planet being kept with who knows how many other women. They won't tolerate your smart mouth." He disappeared inside.

She stared through blurred eyes straight ahead at the forest behind the house. She could run. Disappear in the woods. Freedom was a short distance from here. How far could she get? All the way, maybe? She rose and strolled toward the grove of trees until she was a good distance from the house and ran. The grueling pain in her ankle protested. She didn't give in to it. Her life depended on getting away.

**

He used the key Patterson had given him this morning when he left for the clinic. The room was empty. He shucked his jacket and went to take a shower. The hot water felt wonderful and washed away the smell of animals and antiseptic. When he closed his eyes, her face appeared. Where was she? Did Ran forgive her and take her with him? He opened his eyes and shook the image away. It wasn't any concern to him. She made her decision. He would chalk it up as another bad choice.

He found a clean pair of jeans and a Polo and dressed. Strolling into the sitting area, bare footed, he noticed a bottle of whiskey sitting on the counter. Good old Rex. He poured himself a drink and sipped. Outside, the sun was beginning to set and all the lights of the strip glowed. This was one convention he would never forget. It would be imbedded in his memory. The right woman would come along, and he would fall in love again. His eyes widened as he choked on his drink. He had fallen in love with her.

"There you are. How'd it go at the clinic?" Rex stood in the doorway.

Justin set the glass on the table and stared at it. "It was the most sickening thing I have ever had to deal with. We took care of the critical ones and the few that were left had minor injuries. A doctor will be with them around the clock for the next few days. After that they will be evaluated. Not all of them are going to make it. Some are just too far gone mentally and physically. It's a sick world that treats animals like that, brother." He looked up at Rex. "Where have you been?"

Rex took a seat. "I went with the agents to search the house, see if we could find De Luca's hideout. We didn't find that but we did find the location of the house where he keeps the girls he trucks in for prostitution. Several of the Warlords have been picked up and none of them seem to know where he is either. Or they're not telling." He pitched a large leather bag in Justin's lap.

"What's this?"

"It belongs to Mara. I think it's her safety net. Everything she might need if she had to run away in a hurry," Rex said.

Justin dug in the bag and pulled out several items, including the phone. He turned it on and pulled up the web searches and thumbed through. The Garrett Quarter Horse Ranch came up and he inhaled.

"Mara was the one who sent me the email about you," Rex said.

"I knew she didn't go with him voluntarily." Justin leaned forward.

"She could have put her own life in jeopardy to help you." Rex went to the kitchenette and returned with the bottle of whiskey. He filled Justin's glass and then his own. "Changing the subject, I want to say that I'm sorry about this morning. You're right. You're a grown man and no one has the right to tell you what to do. I guess it's just that I've been the older brother, protecting the baby of the family so long, it's hard to stop."

"I've depended on you and Carson for back-up all my life. I think, deep down, I wanted to stand on my own two feet but was scared. After Mara saved my life and I got to know her, I was amazed how strong and independent she is. She has been alone and taking care of herself since she was a teen. I can't even buy a car without asking yours or Carson's opinion. I don't want to live that way anymore. If I screw up, then I'll learn from my mistakes."

"You fell for her, didn't you?"

He wanted to deny it but this was the new Justin. "Hard."

"We'll find her, if she's alive. But when we do, she may be part of this operation and have to go to jail with the rest of them."

The muscles in his back tightened. His first instinct was to defend her. Her recent actions didn't add up to her being a criminal. "Why would she risk breaking into a warehouse if she was part of it? It was her idea to make a copy and send it to you after she learned you were with the FBI. I just don't think she is part of it." He held up the phone. "This proves it." He swallowed the liquor and stood. "I think I'm going to bed. It's been a rough day."

"Before you go, I need to bring you up to date on a few things."

Justin stopped at the door.

"I'm going to stay and help the agents here as much as I can. It's their case and I don't want to step on toes but they insisted. They're going through the county records for any other property De Luca owns, personally or through a shell corporation, in case there's an address for where he's hiding. He may have left the country altogether. His wife and family are in Italy. There's nothing left for you to do here. You can take the plane back to the ranch so Mom will stop worrying. Thomas can come back after me when I'm ready to leave."

Thomas had worked for the Garrett's for a number of years as ranch foreman. Justin had never learned to fly like his brothers. It didn't appeal to him.

"Okay. I'll leave tomorrow. I'm exhausted."

***

Mara ran deeper into the woods, shoving limbs and briars out of her way. She didn't care that where she was going as long as it was away from the house. She heard running water and picked up her pace. If she got back to Vegas, she would go to Dixie and get her bike. She could ride to Texas. At least she had a plan. She barged through a clearing and a raging river separated her from the other side and freedom. What should she do now?

She was in excellent shape and knew she could outrun the overweight Dagger, but her ankle and the river might be her undoing. She tested the water. Ice cold. If she tried to swim, hyperthermia would cause her death if the river didn't. She wanted to live long enough to see Ran behind bars. She trudged along the river's edge, burying her boots half way up in the mud. If Dagger was tracking her it would be easy for him to see her foot prints. She walked in the shallow area of the water, hoping the water would cover her prints. If she stayed close to the river she stood a better chance of getting away by diving in.

She spotted smoke over the trees in the distance. A steady black stream curled into the sky. She didn't leave the edge of the stream but kept a close watch on the smoke and made her way toward it.

The river dipped and she heard a roar that grew louder the closer she came. Her ankle gave way and her foot slipped down the embankment. She screamed and grabbed for a small tree jutting out of the side of the muddy cliff. It broke off in her hand. Her head collided with a rock and she fell down the embankment and the swirling river swallowed her. She grabbed at boulders and logs searching for anything she could hold on to. The cold water pulled her under, surrounding her in darkness. Her eyes burned and her lungs begged for air. Would this be where her life ended? The water pulled at her body and she didn't know which way was up. She stopped fighting. What was the use? She couldn't compete with the rapids. Her body went limp as the water dragged her down again and her boot hit the bottom. With a solid push, she popped out the top and gulped for air. She tried to scream but coughed water instead. Her head sank under again and she flung her arms above her, searching for anything she could grab to keep from going over the falls. A hand gripped her wrist and pulled her from the murky water.

Her body slid across mud and rotten leaves and she came to rest face down at the edge of the falls. She gasped for breath and couched up water.

"Easy there, Buttercup. Spit it out and you'll be fine."

Chapter 21

Dagger threw her over his shoulder. Darkness had closed in by the time they arrived at the house. Ran stood at the island in the kitchen when they entered through the back door. His hand rose as soon as Dagger set her down. The biker grabbed his arm and twisted it behind him. Dagger stood two feet above the older man and was twice his weight. He pressed his face close to Ran's and growled his threat. "If you ever hit her again, I'll kill you with my bare hands. Real men don't beat women."

She knew he meant every word and Ran did, too. He lowered his arm, glared at her, and stormed out. Dagger helped her into the bathroom. He turned on the shower and started undressing her. She laid her hand over his.

"Thanks. I can do this." He left and closed the door.

She stripped and stepped into the shower. The water stung the cut on her head. Her fingers found the bump and came away with blood mixed with mud. She endured the pain and washed the wound clean. After getting the rest of the mud off, she grabbed a towel and wrapped it around her.

A duffle bag sat on the end of the bed. She rummaged through it and located a pair of her jeans and a sweatshirt with *Diva* in sequins written across the front. It had seemed funny at the time she bought it, now it was just sad. Dagger must have thrown her clothes into the bag before they left the house. She just wished he would help her escape. Why couldn't he have let her go at the river? Told Ran he hadn't been able to find her. Her life was over anyway.

She pulled the blue and white comforter back and crawled into bed. Her body ached and her heart hurt. She longed to feel his arms wrapped around her. To hear the steady beating of his heart next to her chest. To have his fingers massage her sore muscles and whisper in her ear that everything would work out. Tears welled in her eyes, and she released the sobs that had been building for the past eight years. Exhaustion overcame her and she fell asleep.

The constant pounding in her head woke her. A light peeked around the curtains next to the bed. The sun was up. She had slept all night, but her body didn't feel like it. The pounding started again and she realized someone was banging on the door. She threw the covers back and tried to move her legs. The muscles resisted and pain shot up her back. She moaned and forced her body to move and opened the door.

"In the living room, right now!" Ran walked away.

"Where's Dagger?" She called after him.

He didn't turn around. "He's gone."

Her stomach had rocks weighing her down. She looked around the room. She needed a weapon that she could conceal. The armoire held nothing but dust. She checked the dresser and came up empty. The nightstand nearest the door didn't have anything but a couple of paperbacks. The other nightstand had a pen and tablet. She stuffed the pen in her pocket and lifted the tablet. Underneath was a small pair of scissors. Better to be prepared.

She entered the living room. A fire roared in the fireplace giving off a warmth that didn't satisfy the chill running through her. She stood at the door and crossed her arms defiantly. Now that he was safe she wouldn't take anymore crap by choice. Ran had lost his leash over her.

He sat behind a desk with a laptop open in front of him. He motioned with his hand to the two chairs facing the desk.

She ventured forward and sat in one of the leather chairs. Her fingers curled around the scissors in her pocket.

He closed the computer and stared at her. It seemed like hours before he spoke. She could hear her heart pounding in her ears but she didn't break eye contact. He was playing her. She would not be intimidated and lose her composure. Something she had plenty of practice doing.

"You are scheduled to leave this evening. The sheik has called wondering where you are. You were supposed to be on the plane last night, but we know why that didn't happen. If you run again I will kill you and tell your buyer that you took your own life. I have others I can sell. I may not get the money he paid for you, but you're turning out to be more trouble than you're worth. So, you will *not* run. Do you understand?"

"Where's Dagger?"

He shrugged. "He took his bike and left last night."

She continued to glare at him.

He rose and walked around to the front of the desk and sat on the edge. "I can assure you, I did nothing to him. We spoke briefly after you went to bed and he stormed out. When I got up this morning, he was gone. Now, go fix us something to eat."

She stood and walked toward the open door. "I'm not your cook. Fix it yourself." She went back to the bedroom and fell across the bed. She was stuck. If she tried to run, he would send the other bikers after her and with Dagger gone he would take out his frustration on her. Tonight she would be on a plane, bound for slavery. It would be the next chapter in her miserable life.

Chapter 22

The sun beamed through the window next to his bed. He had left the curtains open and spent most of the night watching the flashing lights on the strip. He missed her. Her cool fingers caressing his naked body. Her tender mouth playing tongue tag with his own. Her slender body next to him as they slept. Where could she be? He supposed it didn't matter. She had made her choice. He had to stop obsessing.

He threw the covers back and went to take a shower. He dressed and entered the sitting area. Rex stood at the kitchen counter pouring coffee.

"Want some?"

He nodded and picked up a cup. Rex filled it and Justin dumped half of the dark liquid out and added vanilla creamer to the top. He grabbed a donut from the box and sat on the sofa.

"I want to check on the animals and I'll go to the airport this evening. Will Thomas be ready?"

Rex joined him. "Yes. He'll be there. He went to the casinos last night then slept on the plane. He's ready when you are." He set his cup on the coffee table. "Tell me about Mara."

Justin stared out the window. "Why? What's the point?" He hesitated. "I'm not sure we'll find her. When she wouldn't tell the cops she was being held hostage, I was confused. I thought she couldn't leave her lifestyle behind. But since you found the phone, all that has changed. I wish there was something I could do before anything happens to her."

"From what you've told me she's not someone who would be a party to these crimes but a woman trapped in a life she doesn't know how to get out of."

He ran his hand through his uncombed hair. "She made bad choices. I gave her a way out and she went with him. I still don't believe it was her own choice."

"Sometimes it's just not that simple. When you have been beaten down your whole life, you're afraid things are too good to be true. She's probably traumatized, maybe to the point of PTSD. In cases like this the victim figures the devil you know is better than the devil you don't." Rex stood and filled his cup. "Don't jump to conclusions, bro. You haven't heard her explanation. She may or may not have a good reason for what she did."

"It doesn't matter. When I get on that plane I'll leave her and her memory behind." He leaned forward on the sofa. "There is something else I want to tell you."

"About this case?"

"No. It has nothing to do with the case. When I get home, I'm building a small animal clinic at the entrance of the ranch."

Rex started to speak and Justin raised his hand to stop him.

"I'm using my money and taking nothing from the ranch. I've wanted to help small animals for a long time and realized how much when I worked with the dogs yesterday. I believe I can be an asset to animal control when they rescue those defenseless animals. I'll still take care of the horses, but I'll have the clinic as well. There are plenty of people in our area who have pets that need attention or vaccinations and Tyler is over thirty miles away."

"You've never said anything before. Why now?"

"It's always been in my head and I took several courses to learn as much as I could. You and Carson have drilled it into me that I needed to be a large animal doctor. I don't mind working with the larger animals but my heart is with the smaller ones."

Rex patted his back. "I'm sorry. I never realized you may have had dreams of your own. You should do what pleases you, not me or Carson. If that's what makes you happy, you will have my support and I'm sure Carson will agree."

Justin left a few minutes later for the animal clinic. The receptionist smiled and buzzed him into the back. He knew the way to the holding room.

Doctor Tam greeted him as soon as he opened the door. "Doctor Garrett. Nice to see you." He snapped off his rubber glove and stuck out his hand.

"If it's okay with you, I'd like to check on number twenty-four and thirty-eight. I'll be leaving for Texas this evening and I'll rest easier knowing their condition."

"I'm afraid number twenty-four didn't make it. His heart gave out on him early this morning. You know it can happen sometimes with older animals. I'm guessing they used him strictly for studding. I think the chaos the other night was all too much for him. I'm sorry, I know you did everything you could. Thirty-eight is expected to make a full recovery." Doctor Tam started walking toward the kennels lining a back wall.

Bile rose in his throat. The loss of even one saddened him. Maybe healing most of the dogs was a longshot. Anger like he had never experienced replaced the sadness. His fury was directed toward all those who had had a hand in the animal's death. He tamped his rage down. "That amazes me about animals. They snap back so much faster than humans. Wish we had their secret." He reached the kennel and release the latch. The groggy animal was being kept on pain meds for his own good. He examined him with little resistance. "Good boy." He shut the cage door gently when he finished.

Doctor Tam approached him. "Would you come into my office? I have a matter I'd like your opinion on."

***

The banging on her door woke her. "Time to go. Get a move on. Leave that crap you call clothes. You won't need anything but a burka where you're going." His cruel laugh faded as he walked away.

She crawled out of bed and slipped into her jeans and shirt. She ran a brush through her hair and slammed it on the dresser. It was dark outside. She wasn't too keen on flying in the first place, but flying at night was a phobia for her. She wiped her sweaty hands on her jeans.

Chapter 23

Justin rode the cab back to the hotel to gather his things, and then left for the terminal designated for private planes. Thomas hadn't arrived yet. Justin had called him, not wanting to ruin his good time, but he was anxious to get away from Las Vegas after all that had happened. Thomas said he was in a poker game that should wrap up in thirty or forty minutes and he'd be over afterward.

"That's fine. I'll sit around until you get here. Are you winning?" he chuckled.

Thomas lowered his voice. "About fifty grand."

He found a chair that looked out over the tarmac and saw three private planes. One belonged to the ranch. Another was a jet made for long hops. The other was a smaller plane, most likely some CEO's ride. He went to the soda machine and bought a Coke. He knew from past experience that planes were not allowed to sit on the tarmac for long periods. Curiosity kept his eyes glued out the window. He could see shadowy figures moving inside the larger plane.

Twenty minutes later a Range Rover pulled up close to the largest plane. No one got out. It idled for a long time before the door opened and a tall muscular man in a leather vest opened the back door.

Justin moved closer to the window. His stomach felt like someone had punched him in the gut. His back tightened as another biker got out of the back. They were trying to coax someone out. The first biker stuck his hand inside, jerked it back and yelled a string of curses. He slammed his fist on top of the vehicle. The man reached inside and grabbed a woman and pulled her out by her hair. She swung her arms and legs and kicked his shins until he pinned her down. The other guy latched onto her legs.

They started hauling her to the plane. She fought hard. A night light struck her face and Justin screamed, "Mara!"

He dropped the Coke and threw open the emergency door. Alarms blared. He raced down the stairs to the tarmac. He hurled his whole body onto the back of the biker holding her arms. The guy dropped her and fell across the hood of the Range Rover. The other biker dropped her feet and came after him. Mara was kicking and screaming wildly. She struck one of the bikers in the groin sending him to his knees on the concrete. Justin grabbed her, pulling her up with his good arm. They ran toward his plane. If he could just get there he could lock them in. The bikers were getting closer. The Cessna wasn't far, but he wasn't sure they would make it. He heard the gunshot ding the side of the other plane. As they approached the ranch's plane, the steps to the cabin door lowered to the pavement. Thomas stood in the doorway holding an assault rifle.

"Stop right there, gentlemen." He positioned the gun to his shoulder and pointed it at the men. "These two are coming on this plane and we are taking off. Airport security, the FBI, and the police are on their way. You come any closer and I will shoot and let them clean up the mess." He stepped aside and let Justin and Mara enter.

The bikers stopped and backed away, hands held high. They ran to the Range Rover and screeched away.

Justin helped her to a seat. He pulled her roughly into his arms. "Are you all right?" Her body shook so hard it was all he could do to hold her. Heavy sobs wracked her. She crossed her arms tight around her middle and hung her head.

"Mara talk to me."

She inhaled and raised her head. "Jack Daniels."

Thomas handed her the flask he always carried. She chugged on it, leaned her head against the seat, and closed her eyes.

Justin buckled her up and took the seat next to her. The engine throttled up and the plane moved out to the runway. The sin city lights faded as the plane took to the air.

She didn't speak for a long time. "Where are you taking me?"

Her voice startled him. "Texas."

She sighed and had a faraway look in her eyes. "I've never been to Texas."

He took her hand. "You will love it. There's no desert where we live. There are trees, lakes, mountains, and grass. Lots and lots of grass. I can't wait to show you."

"Ran will find me. I think he killed Dagger. He went against him last night."

Doubts clouded his mind. Didn't she want to leave Las Vegas? She talked about Dagger a lot. He gripped the cushion of the seat to stop his hands from shaking. "Did you love him?"

Her eyes glazed as she stared out the small window. "No. But I'll miss him."

She sniffed. He reached for the box of Kleenex and set it in her lap. She wiped her nose and eyes. He placed his hand on her arm. "It's over now. We'll be in Texas soon. We can put the past behind us."

She shook her head. "You don't understand. I can't outrun my past."

His heart ached for her. "You need to get away from here and all the bad memories. If you don't like Texas or the ranch, I'll buy you a ticket anywhere. I don't want to make you feel like you have to stay. You're a free woman and can do whatever you want."

A sickening laugh ripped from her chest. "Oh, sure. I'll go to Rio or Atlantic City and strip for a living."

"You could go to school."

She turned to face him. "And learn what? How to be a good secretary and make minimum wage for the rest of my life? No thanks."

A phone rang from the cockpit. Justin leaned into the aisle and looked around the seats then sat back.

"It's not like you have to decide your future right now. You've been through a lot in the past forty-eight hours. You're safe now and you don't need to think about it."

"I know—"

Thomas stood in the cockpit door. "That was Rex. I told him you had the girl and he said we have to turn around. He'll meet us at the airport."

He landed the plane, taxied back to the tarmac, and shut the engine. The larger plane had left.

She laid her head against the seat and closed her eyes. He rose after he heard her even breathing. Why would Rex not want them to leave? The question ate at him. He walked to the back of the plane and found a Coke in the fridge. He sipped the soda and stared out the window.

Thomas joined him and grabbed a Coke. "Did Rex say why he wanted us to wait for him?"

Thomas shook his head. "Maybe he's heading back with us. Guess we'll find out."

Fifteen minutes later the cabin door opened and Rex entered, followed by two men wearing dark suits.

"What's going on?" Justin addressed his brother.

One of the agents stepped around Rex. "We have an arrest warrant for Mara Newman."

Chapter 24

Justin rode with Rex and they followed the car with Mara in it.

Rex didn't take his eyes off the road despite Justin's insistent questions and outburst. "Her name is on the disc. She's either heavily involved in the organization or she knows a lot more than she's told you. They are going to question her. It's a material witness warrant. They're giving her the benefit of the doubt at least. She can't go anywhere right now though." Rex said.

At FBI headquarters Justin was told he could wait in the break room. He didn't see where they took her. He couldn't sit and so he paced. Picking up a Styrofoam cup, he poured coffee from the pot and dumped sugar until the coffee overflowed. He poured the mess down the sink, walked to the door, and looked down the hall. He stepped out and yelled, "Rex! Rex Garrett."

A door at the far end opened and his brother walked out. He stormed down the hall and stood in front of Justin. "You can't—"

He grabbed the front of Rex's shirt and yanked him forward. "Don't tell me what I can't do. I want to see her. Did you read her rights? Tell her she has a right to an attorney?"

Rex brushed his hand aside. "Calm down and stop over reacting. This is not my case. I'm only observing. Apparently this is not her first arrest. She knew the drill."

His words only succeeded in fueling the flame. Justin walked around him and headed for the closed door.

"Justin. You can't go in there."

"You watch me." He was going to see her and would demand to be present while they interrogated her. The door opened before he reached it.

"Come in, Mr. Garrett." One of the agents who had taken her off the plane held the door open.

She sat on one side of a long table. Her face was marred with tear stains, her eyes red and swollen. He went around the table, put his arm on her shoulder, and looked up at the three agents. "She wants an attorney."

She put her hand on his arm. "They're not charging me, Justin. They just want my testimony."

The tallest of the three agents pulled out a chair. "Have a seat, Mr. Garrett. We believe her name is used as a cover for De Luca. He was skimming money from the organization and didn't want the Warlords to know. So he used Mara's name to siphon off the money."

"Now that you have her statement, can we leave?"

The agent shuffled his pad into a folder and stood. "I'm afraid that's not possible. We need her here for identity purposes at the moment. We can talk about her leaving and returning for the trial later. When we have De Luca in custody."

Rex walked around the desk and stood next to him. "The agency will put her in protective custody with around the clock guards. I think you should go back to the ranch and I'll keep you updated."

Justin glared at him. "I'm not leaving her."

***

Mara didn't realize she had been holding her breath. She let it out with relief. She wanted him to stay but didn't want to ask. If the Warlords found her, she would end up in the desert like Justin. The only difference, there wouldn't be anyone to save her.

Rex and the tall agent named Greg took them to a small house in a quiet neighborhood. The sparsely furnished house had no pictures on the walls and nothing that indicated someone lived there. A small television sat in the corner on a table.

Justin stood beside her and raised an eyebrow. "Nice."

She had a sudden urge to kiss him but was interrupted by the agent who followed them inside. "I think you'll be comfortable here. There's food in the kitchen. The cable works.

Rex will be sleeping in one of the bedrooms. You and Mara each have a room."

She took his arm. "We'll be in the same room."

Rex chuckled.

The agent cleared his throat. "I'll leave y'all to work out the sleeping arrangements. I'm going to check the perimeter." He left, closing the front door behind him.

The trio settled in the living room. The tension was as thick as a desert sand storm.

She wanted him, alone. To have his arms around her, comforting her, loving her. When Rex spoke, she jumped and he pulled her close.

"Mara, there is something that has been bothering me. Do you mind answering a few more questions?"

A chill ran over her. "Not at all."

He pulled out his pen and pad and flipped it open. "How long did you work at the yard where the records were kept?"

She tucked her hair behind her ear. "A little over a year."

He wrote on the paper. "What were your duties?"

"I answered the phone, wrote up orders, anything Ran asked me to do."

"Who did the job before you?"

"I never met her and when I asked him what happened to her, he said she left."

"Did you have access to the drives?"

She grinned. "Oh, yeah. All the time. I had to record where the merchandise went, to whom, and the money amount."

He took longer to write before asking his next question. "How many people were allowed to see those files?"

"Ran was very picky about who could see them. Three of us had access. Me, Ran, and Dagger."

"Dagger?"

She nodded. "Dagger and Ran were together long before I moved to the house."

Justin spoke. "Dagger disappeared the night before they took her to the airport."

"I think Ran killed him." Mara brushed her hand across her forehead.

Justin went to the kitchen and brought her a cold bottle of water. She stared at his profile and heat surged through her. Her desire for the handsome veterinarian overwhelmed her.

Rex pocketed his pen and pad. "Thanks, Mara. If I think of anything else, I'll let you know." He stood and yawned. "I'm going to bed. I'll see you in the morning."

Justin took her hand, she set the water on the coffee table and let him lead her into another bedroom. A dim light glowed from the lamp beside the bed. He pulled her to the bed and gently pushed her back against the spread. Her body sank into the soft mattress and she pulled him to her.

"I was so afraid I had lost you." He kissed her softly and ran his hand up her ribs to her breasts. She moaned, pulled his head closer and devoured his mouth.

He slipped the leather jacket off and pulled the tank top over her head. His hand found the clasp of her black lace bra and unhooked it releasing her breasts. Her nipples were hard and tender from pressing the inside of her bra. As soon as his mouth covered it, she threw her head back and raised her chest for him.

"I want your hot body naked against me."

He shed his clothes and took his time pulling her leather pants off. His hands roamed over every inch of her. He drove her crazy. "I want you."

He kissed her stomach. "Not this time. I'm going slow and taking you higher than you've ever been."

And he did.

Chapter 25

"I miss you. Trish misses you, too. When are you coming home?"

Rex had adopted Trish, his wife's daughter from a previous marriage and he loved the little girl. "I hope to be home next week. Everything okay there?"

Jamie sighed. "Yep. This house is way too big for two people."

"How are Mom and Amy?" His sister-in-law was very pregnant and past her due date.

"Amy's miserable but she won't slow down. Mrs. G is Mrs. G. That woman is a real pepper. When you get knitted socks this Christmas, you *will* wear them."

A knock on his door interrupted their conversation. "I have to go, baby. I love you and I'll see you soon. Kiss my girl for me." He disconnected and yelled, "Yes?"

"We're hungry. We want to go to a restaurant and eat breakfast," Justin called out through the door.

He opened the door. "I don't think it's a good idea for either of you to leave the house until De Luca is captured. Mara is a threat to him and he has too many people he can send after her. I'll have one of the agents go pick up something."

Mara entered the room and stood next to him. She dropped her head.

"Sorry, Mara. No matter how much we want De Luca, our first concern is your safety."

"I know. It seems I've been a prisoner in some way or another all my life. I want to go out and do… something"

Justin took her in his arms. "You're not a prisoner. I'll order breakfast. What do you want?"

***

Rex left the pair a short time later. They had eaten breakfast at the small table in the kitchen and were finishing their coffee, having nowhere else to go.

He talked about the ranch, his mom, and his plans to open a small animal clinic. He was running out of small talk and trying to keep her from thinking about her dilemma when she surprised him with a question.

"Do you have a girlfriend in Texas?"

He thought about Samantha. She was a dedicated U.S. Marshal. They had dated for nine months before he terminated the relationship. It never would have worked. He might have been selfish to want her to stay home more, and she had her goal set on a DC position. Her job required her to travel all over the world, and he didn't know where she was most of the time. It turned out to be a mutual agreement and they ended up being good friends. "Nope."

"Why not?"

He laughed to lighten the mood, but she looked serious. "That's a silly question. I haven't met anyone I wanted to have a long-term relationship with."

Chills ran over her. She grabbed her stomach and held her breath to keep from losing her breakfast. "I don't feel well. I think I'll lie down." She rose abruptly, almost knocking over the chair. She went to the bedroom where they had spent most of the night making love. That was a joke. They had sex. Love had nothing to do with it.

What was happening? How could he have said he hadn't met the right one? She had hoped. It didn't matter now. He didn't care for her the way she did for him.

She crawled on the bed and hugged the pillow, inhaling his spicy scent. She didn't want to be here. Maybe she should insist he go back to Texas without her. She would have to assure him everything would be fine. He believed he was here to protect her. She had learned a long time ago how to protect herself and didn't need him or anyone else. Where had all this 'protection' been when she was ten and being molested? Or when she had been thrown out in the street? Or when Ran had been beating the hell out of her?

She couldn't stay cooped up. She slipped into her leather jacket, pulled on her boots, and shoved a baseball cap on her head. She had to get out of this house. Get the hell away from all these people and their overly helpful ways. They were using her just like everyone else. The Feds wanted her testimony, Justin wanted her body, and Ran wanted her dead. If she disappeared well enough, no one could use her again. She quietly opened one of the bedroom windows that looked out onto the backyard. She watched from the shadows of the bedroom as two agents walked across the grass, patrolling. She checked the clock next to the bed. Fifteen minutes later the same pair strolled into view again. She had a fifteen minute window to run. She pushed out the screen, planted her booted foot, firmly on the nightstand, and scrambled through the opening.

Running through the backyards of the subdivision wasn't a big deal. These were modest homes with well-trimmed yards and few trees. The last house on the block backed up to a busy road, and she was able to hail a cab.

She had always loved the Forum Shops at Caesars. She stepped out of the cab into the hustle and bustle of people. In her younger days she used to take shelter here when the weather turned ugly and spent hours gazing through the windows until security kicked her out. When Ran began wooing her while she still worked at The Pink Titty, he would bring her here and buy her beautiful things. Balenciaga, Burberry, Jimmy Choo, were her favorites. He threw money around like he never ran out just to impress her. And sadly, it had. She strolled up and down the walkway looking in the windows. She stopped at Bebe's. A black leather dress in the window caught her eye. It had a see-through lace midriff and was accented with funky rhinestones. She wanted it, bad. She walked in and asked to try it on. In the dressing room she slipped the dress over her head. Turning left and right, she admired how well it showed off her figure. She had to have it.

"How does it fit?" Mara opened the door and showed the sales girl who looked vaguely familiar.

"It is so cute. Did I see a pair of heels in the window that would match?"

The young blonde girl smiled. "What size?"

She slipped her bare feet into the black lace pumps that matched the dress. Rhinestones covered the heels.

"Let me show you something." The blonde left and returned with two rhinestone daisies and clipped them onto the top of the shoes.

"Oh, how awesome." Mara beamed.

"The shoes are half price this week." The saleswoman looked toward the door for the second time. She brought more accessories for Mara to play around with.

Mara finally decided on the dress, the shoes, and the clips. She handed the clerk a few hundreds and told her she would wear the outfit. The girl headed toward the register with her old clothes.

"That dress was made for you, I totally love it," the clerk remarked as she bagged Mara's clothes she wore in.

"I do, too." A familiar voice interrupted the two women.

Mara immediately recognized the male voice coming from behind her. "Dagger." She threw her arms around his neck and squeezed him. "I thought you were dead. Where did you go? I was so worried."

"I'm fine. A little bird told me you were here. How are you?"

She looked at the clerk, who seemed to be trying to control a smile as she rang up the sale. That's why she looked familiar, she had seen her buying drugs at the Warlord's clubhouse. "The FBI has me locked in a house in Green Valley. They have guards posted everywhere, and said no one can find me. I got bored and decided to take a little break."

Dagger leaned close and whispered in her ear. "I just found you. You see, you're not so safe after all. I can protect you. Why don't you come with me?"

The clerk retreated to another part of the store leaving the pair alone. Mara looked toward the entrance of the mall. It was void of people for the most part as the lunch hour approached. The crowd had ventured into the casino. She didn't know if she was ready to give up on Justin, even though he didn't care for her the way she cared for him. This could be a way for her to disappear, but something inside her pulled against her leaving with Dag. "All I have to do is start screaming and there will be FBI agents here in five minutes. I'll be fine."

He put his hand on her arm and raised his brows. "I think you might be interested when I tell you who I've located."

She squinted and looked up at him. "There's not anyone I can think of who I care to see."

He caressed her cheek. "Oh yes, you do. I've located a relative of yours, and she is anxious to meet you. No one knows about her but me. She's not far from here, and you'll be safe there."

Her heart jumped in her throat. She and Dagger had had lengthy conversations about her past. He knew she didn't think she had any family left. She had confided to him that there must be grandparents somewhere, but she had no idea where to look. Research into her past always came to a dead end until she finally gave up. "Who, Dag?"

"Her name is Margaret Waters. She's your paternal grandmother and wants to meet her only granddaughter."

***

Justin sat up and looked around. It took him a few seconds to remember his location. He rubbed his face and rose. He checked the bedroom door and found it locked.

"Mara." She didn't answer. He knocked. "Mara. Are you awake?"

After several attempts get her to open the door, he became worried. He had an empty feeling in his stomach and his mouth was bone dry. He kept knocking and calling her name. The only reason she wouldn't answer is if she was hurt, or worse.

He finally grew so desperate that he kicked the door. The cheap wood and old lock were no match for his boot. The door flew open.

He stared at the empty bed. The curtains waved in the breeze coming from the open window. He checked the bathroom. He rushed through the rest of the house, checking every room. "Mara," he yelled over and over.

He searched for his cell phone and found it charging on the counter. He punched in Rex's number.

"Justin, I'm in the middle of an interrogation. Can I call you back?"

"She's not here."

He heard a chair scrape across a floor. "What? Are you talking about Mara?"

He ran his hand across his face. "Yeah. She's gone."

"What did the agents outside say? Did they see her leave?"

He tried not to scream into the phone. "I have no idea."

"Okay. Slow down. Tell me what happened."

He explained that she hadn't felt well and went to lie down. He had gone to sleep and when he awoke she was gone.

"Go outside and check with Gary, the agent who is supposed to be in charge. Go, now. Don't hang up," Rex ordered.

He ran outside and found three agents standing by an SUV, smoking. "Mara's missing. Have you seen her?"

The one he assumed was Gary threw his cigarette on the ground, grabbed his jacket, and pushed past Justin. He followed Gary through the house while he searched every corner and closet.

"Let me talk to him." Justin had almost forgotten Rex on the phone.

He passed the phone to the agent.

"The girl's not here. Looks like she left under her own steam through a window in the bedroom. I'll go look around, knock on some doors to see if anyone saw anything. I know this is my screw-up. I'll call as soon as I know something." He handed the phone back to Justin.

He listened to his brother's order. "Don't leave the house. I'll be there in a few minutes."

Justin sat on the sofa and rested his head in his hands. "Where would she go? Why would she leave?"

Chapter 26

The excitement raging through her body made her want to scream with joy. What would she be like? Would they like each other? Why did her father never mention his mother? Did she hate him? Was he a rebel when he was a teen and they kicked him out? She could relate to that.

He drove in silence. She needed this time to think about the woman who was her only living relative. Or the only one she knew about. Did her father have any siblings? She might have aunts or uncles.

The city fade into dry, desolate desert. The hair on the back of her neck stood up. "Where are we going?" she asked.

He didn't take his eyes off the road ahead. "It's not far."

"She doesn't live out here in the desert, does she?" They hadn't passed a town or house for a while. Nothing but dark, flat land dotted with an occasional cacti. People couldn't get water and would have to drive miles for food. Something was definitely wrong.

His jaw clenched. "She lives near Laughlin. We should be there in about twenty minutes. I have to make a stop first."

He pulled off the main highway and they traveled down a dusty road. He followed it in between two mountains to a flat open area with an abandoned town where he stopped. The road continued through the town and disappeared into the mountains in the distance. She could feel the blood drain from her face. She froze, rooted to the seat. Her heart raced.

"Get out," he ordered. His gentle tone from earlier had disappeared.

Several Warlords stepped out onto the decaying porch of what looked like an old hotel. Ran walked between them. She gasped.

Her body tensed and perspiration trickled down between her breasts. She swiped at her cleavage and wiped her hand on the seat. She opened her door and placed her new heels on the ground. "What are we doing here, Dag?" She made an attempt to keep her voice from quivering.

He didn't answer but walked around the vehicle and grabbed her arm, jerking her forward.

She stumbled, her ankle twisted, and the rhinestone heel of her new shoe broke. A sharp pain shot up her leg and she fell in the dirt, landing on a small jagged rock, tearing her dress. She bit her bottom lip as the pain increased. She had landed on the same ankle she had hurt earlier. Dagger startled her when he picked her up as if she weighed nothing, carrying her up on the porch, setting her on a dirty bench.

How could she have been so naïve? She knew better than to put her trust in him. "What's going on, Dag?"

Ran walked out to the steps of the building. "Dagger wants the four million we'll get for you as much as I do." He waved his hand at the rest of the bikers. "They get twenty percent. Dagger and I split the rest. Normally, I'm not so generous, but he deserves a procurement fee, I felt. Although, the money won't clear the account until the merchandise is delivered."

She glared at him. "They said you were in jail."

His sickening laugh sent cold chills over her. "Money can do wonders these days."

A small plane circled over the town and flew low. She looked up. The landing gear lowered and the engines slowed. It touched down thirty feet from the deteriorating hotel.

Dagger grinned. "Your transportation is here."

Chapter 27

Gary Patterson, the agent who let Mara get past him, came inside the house. "Got a lead. A couple of security guards saw someone matching one of the Warlord's description leaving the Forum with a young woman. I think it might be her. They'll have security footage ready for us by the time we get there."

Rex rose from the sofa and Justin followed. The two brothers and three agents rode to Caesar's in silence. Once in the shopping area they were led by a guard down a hallway to the elevator. In the basement Gary knocked on a door marked *Security.*

A young technician sitting behind a number of screens and keyboards addressed the group. "I understand the timeframe is between two and four this afternoon. I've taken the liberty to narrow down the tapes to view an hour before and after."

The agents found spots where they could see, and the tech pushed the buttons for the screens to play. Justin's eyes traveled back and forth, viewing the multiple videos.

He spotted her entering the dress shop. A tall muscular biker walked in a short time later. "Wait. That's Dagger."

All agents watched the multiple screens and saw her in a black leather dress and heels leave with the biker. The tech switched screens to the foyer and front door. The pair walked out of the shopping arcade together. The parking area appeared on another screen and the lights blinked on a dark gray Hummer. They got in and drove away.

Rex grabbed his pad and wrote down the license plate number. "I hate to say it, Justin but it looks like she left with him voluntarily."

The young tech swiveled in his chair. "You can contact LVPD and view the traffic cams. Las Vegas has them posted all the way to the city limits."

Gary opened the front door. "I've already called them. They're waiting for us."

Justin climbed into the backseat of the agency's SUV and they traveled downtown.

"The cameras are on a twenty-four hour loop. We may all have to view different screens from around the city," Gary informed them.

An older woman checked their identification and opened the security door. She set each agent at a screen and keyed in the timeframe they were looking for.

"There's the Hummer. They headed east; toward the desert," one of the agents commented.

Justin stood. He wiped his sweaty hands on his jeans. His heart ready to explode. "Mara said Ran had sold her and he was putting her on a plane. Are there any private landing strips in the desert?"

Gary answered. "Too many. There aren't any major highways or houses until you get to Laughlin except ghost towns." He pointed to the screen showing the Hummer leaving Vegas. He took the paper with the license number from Rex. "I'll put out an APB on the vehicle and order a helicopter. Wallace, contact FAA and see what they have recorded arriving or leaving within a hundred and fifty mile radius. Although it's not like these kind of people to file flight plans, we might get lucky."

From the back seat of the SUV Justin's mind ran all over the map. What if Ran got her out of the country before he found her? How would he locate her then? He pressed his nose with his finger and thumb.

He raised his head as they entered the airport. The sun was sinking. How would they search in the dark? Rex voiced his thoughts to Gary.

"If we don't get up quick, the search will be called off until tomorrow morning."

"What if they have a private plane and take off from a private strip?" Justin asked anxiously.

"That's a good possibility. But we need to stay positive right now," his brother told him.

The helicopter sat on the tarmac ready for the agents. Rex and Justin followed the agents out to load. Gary stopped them.

"He can't go. This is an FBI operation."

Justin stepped forward and Rex caught his arm. "He has seen all these people. None of the agents have. He's going. I'll take full responsibility if there is retribution from the agency."

They climbed in and the helicopter shot up, following the path the camera showed the Hummer had taken. He glued his face to the window. Binoculars were passed to him and he searched the ground. Nothing but cacti, a few small animals, and a cougar. No airstrip or sign of the Hummer. It got to the point where everything on the ground had shadows.

"Look for out-of-the way places with a fire burning or lights on. At night they'll need landing lights," one of the agents told him.

They flew over a shell of a town but didn't see any vehicles, lights or fire. When the chopper swooped low and flashed their search lights over the area again, Justin spotted an object on the ground. The helicopter lights reflected on something that sparkled. It could be a colorful rock or a tin can.

"Can we get any lower?" he asked the pilot through his headset.

The chopper swooped down, blowing sand and setting off a dust storm. He couldn't see the object.

"There's no denying that strip is a runway," Patterson remarked.

"Put it down. I want a closer look," Rex ordered.

The pilot circled and set the helicopter down. The agents hopped out and shots rang out pinging the side of the chopper. The agents drew their weapons. Justin hit the ground and lay flat.

The agents scattered, taking up positions behind buildings. Justin ran for the porch of a two-story structure and ducked beside the steps. He peeped over the top and saw the barrel of a gun sticking through a broken window. The shooter fired another round. He slipped up on the porch and crawled across to the window. Before the shooter could fire another shot, He grabbed the gun barrel and jerked it and the shooter through the window. He pinned him to the ground. Another man bolted through the door and pointed a revolver at Justin's head. "Let him go."

A pistol cocked. He was sure this was the end. A shot was fired, but instead of feeling the hot lead hit his body, the biker dropped onto the porch.

Rex jumped on the porch, cuffing the biker he had pulled through the window. "I told you to stay in the chopper."

He got to his feet. "I'm making my own choices now." He picked up the downed biker's gun and entered the hotel and searched the lower level. The crumbling stairs shook as he ascended to search the upper level. On the floor behind a door he a pair of woman's black shoes. One of the rhinestone heels was missing. She was here. Panic ripped through his body. He rushed downstairs. Loud gunshots were still going off outside. He went toward the back of the building and searched for another way out. A door with peeling gray paint provided an exit, but the door stuck. He braced his foot on the frame, pulled on the knob, and used every ounce of strength he had. The door swung open. He fell backward. For a few seconds he couldn't breathe.

He recovered and scrambled to his feet, ran outside, and rushed to a newer building with large doors. He opened a side door and a shot hit the wall next to him. He dropped to the dirt floor and hid behind some fifty-five gallon drums. Crawling, he got to a spot where he could see the large open area where an airplane sat. He crouched and eased around to the other side of the plane. A gun fired again and hit one of the drums of fuel setting, off an explosion. Flames lit up the dark building catching one side of the wood structure on fire.

The engines of the plane started, the pilot racing to get out of the burning building. Justin picked up the weapon he had dropped and inched his way toward the open door of the plane. A biker stood in the opening while others were trying to put out the flames. He slipped under the plane next to the pull-down stairs. He hit the bottom of the metal craft with the gun. The biker stepped out on the steps to look underneath the plane. Justin held the barrel of his gun and swung, hitting the big man in the face. The biker dropped his gun, covered his face with his hands, and fell to the ground. He hit him again, knocking him out. He raced up the stairs into the plane.

"Mara?"

"You'll never get her out of here. I'll kill both of you first. Drop the weapon."

Chapter 28

"You can't get away, De Luca. The place is surrounded." He gripped the back of the seat closest to him.

The shorter man didn't waver. "I can if that brother of yours wants you back without holes. I said drop the gun."

He let the weapon fall. "Besides the money, what satisfaction do you get out of abusing animals and exploiting women? Forcing young girls into prostitution. I'm just curious what gets an asshole like you off. How do you justify it all?"

Ran stepped closer and grinned. "A lot you know. The animals are throwaways from the streets, walking around as strays or the animal shelters where they are destined for the death penalty. I save them. They get to do what they were bred to do. Fight. They live or die with dignity."

He eased forward a few inches. "So you believe you are rescuing the animals. What about the women and young girls you abduct and turn out on the streets? They get hooked on drugs, contract diseases, are sometimes beaten to death. What about them?"

"They live in dark corners or flop houses, eating out of trash piles before they come to me. I feed them, give them shelter, and put clothes on their backs. They're better off. I can't see how that is a bad thing. I'm doing them a favor."

A low moan come from the back of the plane. Justin looked toward the curtain drawn across the cabin doorway. Ran glanced over his shoulder and he grabbed the barrel of the gun. A loud boom penetrated the close quarters of the cabin, temporarily deafening him. He jerked the gun, still held by his foe. Ran fell forward onto the carpet. Heat burned Justin's hand. He jumped on top of him and twisted his wrist. The gun fell to the floor and Justin grabbed it. He pointed it at his head.

Ran swung his fist, connecting with his jaw, throwing him off balance. The gun went off again and both men froze.

A bright red patch appeared on his white shirt. It got larger and larger. The man's eyes were wide and Justin saw the pain reflected on his face. He stood. The wounded man's labored breathing filled the cabin. Gun fire was getting closer to the building. He couldn't take a chance on going for help. He knelt and ripped the blood stained shirt open. The bullet didn't look like it hit a major organ. He checked Ran's pulse, which raced. The man was scared. He grabbed a jacket thrown over one of the seats and pressed it against the wound.

"I don't think it's going to kill you. Although God knows you deserve it. Hang on and I'll do what I can until help comes. But you need to calm down or you'll have a heart attack."

"Hurry. I don't want to die."

Justin rose and opened the curtain in the back. It was dark. He located a switch on the wall and flipped it. Wall sconces came on and Mara lay on a sofa. He knelt beside her.

"Mara." He touched her bare leg. It was cool but not cold.

"Justin," she whispered weakly.

Rex appeared at the cabin entrance. "Is she alive?"

"She has a weak pulse. I think she's been drugged. I need to get her to the hospital."

"Looks like De Luca needs an ambulance, too."

He couldn't take his eyes off of her. He slipped his good arm under her legs and forced his injured arm under her neck, lifting her off the bed. His pain didn't matter. "We've got to get her to the hospital. I'm not sure what they gave her, but I suspect it was too much."

Rex helped De Luca up and sat him in a seat. "I need to know what you gave her."

"I don't know what you're talking about." De Luca grimaced, clearly not interested in anything but his own pain.

He leaned over the seat and put pressure on his wound. De Luca screamed. Rex spoke softly. "The barn is on fire. There's a meth lab in the back that is going to explode at any moment. I can leave you here or I can get you to the hospital. It depends on what you tell me. You don't have a lot of time."

"Dagger gave her Benzo. I have no idea how much. Now get me out of here."

Rex helped him up, following Justin and an inert Mara out of the plane. They rushed to the helicopter. Justin passed her up to Agent Knolls and climbed in beside her.

***

Once the chopper left for the hospital, Rex skirted the burning building and joined Patterson and Jefferies. They had cuffed the bikers still alive and taken them away from the barn. Several SUVs and vans were loading them to take to jail.

Patterson stepped over to him. "Some of them got away but I've called it in. Hopefully they'll be picked up before they get out of Nevada. How's the girl?"

Rex shook his head. "I don't know. She's unresponsive and her breathing is shallow. Ran admitted they had given her Benzodiazepine. It may be an overdose situation."

"There's another wagon coming for these guys but no need for us to be here. These guys can handle the cleanup. They should be here within the next fifteen minutes. We can take one of these cars and go straight to the hospital, if you want."

"I do."

"It was a good bust. First the dogs and now the meth lab," Gary grinned.

"What about the trafficking? Is there an update on that?"

Gary nodded. "They were using the trucks from that warehouse in town. One truck was found just before it crossed the state line. There were some very frightened young women in the back who will be reunited with their families in Mexico. They were taken to the hospital for detox. The rest we'll keep looking for. Sorry we couldn't tie the whole thing up in a neat bow tonight, but I think we've done well."

Rex took his hat off and ran a hand through his hair. "I'd say it's been a good week."

Headlights flashed on the dirt road. Two vehicles pulled up next to the handcuffed prisoners. The agents put the captured bikers into the back of the van and several agents climbed in with them. After the van pulled away, Rex and the other three agents left. It seemed to take forever to get to the hospital.

Chapter 29

Rex entered the emergency room and showed the receptionist his credentials. "Two people arrived by helicopter a short time ago and I'm searching for my brother, Justin Garrett. He's with a woman who was admitted with a BZD overdose."

"I'll show you where they are."

He followed the nurse through the doors to the emergency ward. Justin was speaking to a doctor who looked at Rex when he entered.

The doctor nodded at him but continued to explain Mara's condition. "Her ankle is fractured but that's minor. How long has she been taking drugs?"

"She's not." He cocked his head. "They were forced on her. Apparently they shot her up with Benzodiazepines. Will she be conscious soon?"

"They gave her too much. She's in a coma."

He stepped closer to the bed and held her hand. "Will she be okay?"

"We're doing everything we can."

An orderly came and wheeled a sleeping woman to the fourth floor. Justin followed the bed. She never stirred. If he could take her place he would. He took her cold hand and ran his thumb across the top. When Rex tapped him on the shoulder he doubled his fist and turned.

Rex raised his hand. "It's just me. You're wound too tight. Why don't you let me take you to a hotel so you can sleep?"

"I'm not leaving her."

Rex sighed. "There's nothing you can do for her. You have to wait for the drugs to get out of her system and that may take a while. If you don't get any sleep, you will be useless to her when she wakes up. Be reasonable."

He ran his hand over the stubble that hadn't seen a razor in two days. He leaned over and kissed her forehead. She looked so innocent. He wanted to hold her. He nodded at Rex.

Rex checked in with the other agents before asking a nurse about De Luca. She informed him that he was stable in the trauma ward, under guard.

He drove the short distance to the Hilton Grand near the University Hospital. After checking in they entered the quiet hotel room. Justin started stripping before making it to the bedroom. "I'm taking a shower."

"You'll need this." Rex held out a bag that contained his clothes and toiletries from the safe house. "I'll order room service. Anything in particular you don't want?"

"I don't care. I'm not really hungry." He closed the bathroom door. After he had shaved and finished his shower he joined his brother.

An assortment of food covered the tiny table. It smelled heavenly and his stomach rumbled.

"Better come join me before I devour it all," Rex said as he stuffed a burger in his mouth.

Justin slid onto the chair across from his brother. He grabbed a bowl of chili and reached for the crackers. He crumbled a whole sleeve into the bowl.

Rex looked at the bowl and then at Justin. "You like a little chili with your crackers?"

He shoved a spoonful of the mix into his mouth and nodded. After he swallowed he addressed the question. "You eat chili how you want and I'll eat the way I want."

"She's going to be all right, bro."

"I don't want her to wake up alone."

***

The sun beamed through the blinds, reflected off of green walls, and caused Mara to squint to focus. A base drum pounded out a steady beat in her head, keeping time with her pulse. She gagged on the disinfectant smell penetrating her nostrils. Her body resisted when she tried to sit up in search of a trash can in case she puked.

She swung her legs over the side of the bed. Her bare feet connected with the cold tile floor while she rested her backside against the bed until the dizziness subsided. Her hand grabbed the tray table and it rolled away. Leaning forward, she pulled it back and braced herself. With effort, she made it into the bathroom and emptied her stomach. She splashed cool water on her face and rinsed her mouth. Now if her head would stop hurting, she could get the hell out of this hospital.

"You're awake."

She stumbled and Justin grabbed her around the waist, helping her to the bed. "Oh, my God. You scared the crap out of me." She tried yelling but it came out as a croak.

"I'm sorry. How long have you been awake?"

She settled on the side of the bed with her feet dangling over. "Not long. I've got to get out of here. I hate hospitals."

"How are you feeling?"

She rubbed her temples. "Like someone is having a wild party in my head. I need Tylenol."

He pressed the call button attached to her bed and a voice come over the intercom.

"May I help you?"

Mara answered. "Can I get something for a headache?"

"I'll check your chart to see what you can have. I'll be in shortly."

She leaned back against the pillow and looked at him. "What happened?"

He pulled a chair closer to the bed and sat. He explained how they had found her and the fire that destroyed the meth lab and the airplane.

"Did you get Ran and Dagger?"

"Ran was shot, treated here, and will be released into custody."

"What about Dagger?"

He took her hand and ran his thumb over the back. "Last I heard, he hadn't been found." He hesitated. "Mara, I shot Ran."

Her eyes widened. "You?"

He nodded slowly.

She placed her hand on the side of his face. "I can't believe you had it in you."

"Are you mad?"

"Are you kidding? Of course not. That bag of shit deserved much worse. It does bother me that Dagger wasn't caught. He and Ran are partners. He's the one who drugged me. He was in on all of it from the start." She looked out the window. She had trusted him to keep her safe. "I thought he was my friend. I'm a lousy judge of character apparently."

He sat up straight and pulled out his cell phone. "That means you are still in danger. I need to let Rex know so they can get you into protective custody."

She grabbed his hand. "I don't want to hide anymore."

The door opened and a nurse brought two pills in a paper cup and handed them to her. "This should help."

"Will they put me to sleep?"

The nurse shook her head. "It's Tylenol."

As soon as the door closed behind the nurse, she squeezed his hand. "Find my clothes and let's get out of here. I want to go to Texas with you. Dagger won't find me there. Please, Justin."

He opened doors until he found the clothes she wore into the hospital. He helped her into the bathroom and she emerged a few minutes later in the leather dress. "I hope they don't wear shoes in Texas."

Chapter 30

Mara's nails dug into the armrest as the Cessna zoomed down the runway and lifted into the air. Her heart rested in her throat. This was only her second time in an airplane. She had vowed never to fly again after the first time. Not having control bothered her. His hand tightened on her arm.

"Are you afraid of flying?"

Her mouth felt like it was stuffed with cotton and she couldn't speak. She nodded.

"I'll get you some water." He disappeared down the aisle and returned with a cool bottle.

She drank half the bottle. "Better. Thank you. Besides our short flight the other day, I've only flown one other time and the damn plane bucked and swayed all over the sky."

"You must have been in a bad storm. The weather should be good on this trip. Thomas said it was seventy-five degrees in Texas today and no rain in sight." His cell buzzed.

His brows creased. His lips formed a thin line as he pressed the button.

"Yeah."

She could hear the party on the other end yelling. This couldn't be good. She placed her hand over her stomach that had suddenly started churning. She couldn't get sick. Although, she didn't remember the last time she had eaten. She tried to hear what the caller was saying but even with the loud voice she couldn't get everything. The drift of most of the conversation was Justin was in serious trouble. He wasn't saying much, just listening and saying yes now and then. She wanted him to wrap up the call so she could learn what trouble he was in. She was with him now and must be part of the trouble. Patience wasn't her best quality.

She sat quietly and waited. It seemed the conversation went on forever. When he finally spoke she understood most of the discussion.

"This is my decision, not yours. Let them come after me. There are no charges filed and as far as I can see she's free to go wherever she wishes to go." He didn't speak for a long time and when he did, it wasn't the man she knew. "You tell them to do what they feel is necessary. They can speak to our attorney whenever they're ready." He disconnected, then turned off the phone. He inhaled deeply and relaxed against the back of his seat and closed his eyes.

"You want to tell me about that?" She asked in a soft voice.

His eyes stayed closed. "That was Rex. It seems we've broken a few laws. The FBI didn't want you or me to leave the state until after the arraignment at the very least. If they want you to testify, then we'll fly back. Simple as that. But I'll contact my attorney as soon as we land."

"Do you think we should go back?"

He seemed to snap out of his musing and took her in his arms. "Not on your life. As far as I'm concerned, we fled because I had reason to believe your life is still in danger and you are in need of protection. I can do that in Texas. Nevada is a wild card; cops on the take; Dagger still on the loose; and nowhere to stay except more safe houses. I'm right on this one. You don't need to worry."

Somehow his words eased her tension. She couldn't ever remember feeling safe. Shifted from home to home with people who were strangers just to get the money the government provided. She didn't see a dentist until she started making her own money. Over-the-counter medicine was all she ever took if she got sick. The last home put her on birth control pills. She soon learned why. The man in the house tried to use her as his personal sex slave. It hadn't been easy on the streets. If she had it to do over, she would have located relatives. Would her life have been different? No way to know. Right now, she was safe. And Justin had provided that.

***

She laid her head against his shoulder. Her even breaths indicated she had fallen asleep. Hopefully, she would sleep until they reached the ranch.

He eased a pillow from the opposite seat and positioned her head on it. He rose and made his way to the rear of the plane where Rex kept a bottle of Jack. He poured a shot and swallowed the amber liquid in one gulp then poured another. Reaching under the counter, he grabbed a few cubes of ice and dropped them into his glass. He swirled them around. The call from Rex weighed heavily on his mind.

His brother had been mad as hell, but he was determined not to give in to either of his brothers again. In Las Vegas he had been at a disadvantage. He would feel more at ease on the ranch. He could protect her if anything happened. It was the right decision to refuse to turn the plane around. He was prepared to go even further if Rex or any of Ran's gang came after her.

He finished the liquor and set the glass in the sink. He headed back to his seat when Thomas stuck his head out of the cockpit.

"Another twenty minutes and we'll be on the ranch. I haven't called your mom since it's so late. Do you want me to wake them up?"

He shook his head. "No. They may hear the plane engines anyway."

"Roger. Take your seat and fasten up." Thomas disappeared into the cockpit.

He rested his head against the seat. All he wanted was a shower and clean clothes. He was sure she would want to change as well. He lifted his head. She had no clothes and it was too late to go shopping. She was about the same size as Amy and Jamie. He took out his phone. Which one should he call? Not Amy. Her baby was due any day and she would go out of her way to help. Jamie would know the necessary things a woman would need.

At first he didn't think anyone would answer. Finally a groggy voice came on the line.

"Hello."

"Hey, Jamie. It's Justin. I'm sorry to wake you, but I need some help."

When she spoke again it sounded like she was more alert. "Sure, Justin. What can I do?"

He explained the situation. Jamie understood and said she would have the things sent down. They would be at his house when the plane landed.

He heard the landing gear lower and the plane began to slow. He shook her gently.

"We're landing. You might want to sit up. I need to buckle you up anyway."

"Are we in Texas?"

"We are and only a few minutes from a hot shower and clean clothes."

She smiled then a frown creased here brow. "I have no clothes."

He caressed her cheek. "You will by the time we land. My sweet sister-in-law is your size and is sending clothes over for you."

"I'll pay her for them." Her lips pressed together.

"Don't worry about anything, Mara. I'll take care of you until you decide what you want to do."

She shook her head. "That's just it, Justin. I have taken care of myself most of my life. I'm not sure I even know how to let someone take care of me. I have no training to speak of." A tear slipped down her cheek.

He covered her hand with his own. "I plan to open a clinic on the edge of the ranch and I'll be needing an assistant. You could go to the local college and take a few courses and I can teach you what they can't. But I'm not trying to make your decision for you. That is up to you. If being an assistant for a vet doesn't appeal to you then you can go in any direction you want. It's your life."

She didn't say anything. The plane landed and Thomas assisted her down the steps and into the white Jeep parked in the hangar. Justin got behind the wheel and Thomas hopped in the back. After dropping Thomas off at the barn where he left his car, he drove to the last house in the horseshoe drive. Out of the corner of his eye he saw her take in the surroundings. He pulled into the carport and walked around to open her door.

He keyed the lights to come on and the house lit up. He unlocked the door and she walked ahead of him.

"This is the dining room in front of the patio doors and the kitchen is on the other side of the bar. There is a guest bedroom to the left and upstairs is the master suite plus two more bedrooms. You have your pick of rooms."

She looked at him like he had grown an extra head. She cocked her head to one side. "Where do you sleep?"

"I'll show you." He took her hand and led her up the stairs to the master bedroom. "This is my domain and here is the bathroom."

She eased an arm around his waist. "This is where I want to sleep. With you."

He couldn't resist the temptation. "Then this is where you will sleep." He lowered his mouth to her waiting lips.

Their clothes flew. He held her hand and pulled her into the large bathroom. A glass shower sat at one end of a Jacuzzi tub. He punched in some numbers to adjust the water temperature and led her into the shower. His lips found hers and their naked bodies melted together. He rained kisses down her neck and to her left breast. The nipple was taunt as he took it into his mouth. She moaned which made him hotter.

Her breath came in short gulps. She pushed on his shoulders. "Stop."

He released her nipple and gazed into her clear blue eyes. Confusion creased his brow.

"Oh, God, I've missed you. The whole time I was chained to that pole in the basement, you were on my mind. It kept me going. I'll live with the scars he left, but he could never beat your memory out of me. I think I've fallen in love with you. I can say it without having to pretend or fake the pleasure you give me. Pleasure, I might add, that I've never had before. You are amazing and have stepped into my heart and soul. I'm afraid I'd have to kill you if you ever considered leaving me. I'll be totally lost in your world. I'm not a farm girl but I will try. You must know I come with many scars. Some are so deep I don't know if they will ever heal."

He held her face in his hands. "Scars are only a reminder of your past. They can cloud your future if you let them." He kissed her damp mouth. "I'm here for the long haul and to make sure those scars don't get in the way of a new beginning."

Her hand gripped his butt and she pulled him closer. She wrapped her legs around his waist and he held her tight in his hands and slipped his hard member inside her. He groaned as her heat surrounded him.

The pounding warm water on his back set his pace and he took her hard and fast. She matched him stroke for stroke until they both collapsed in a heap on the tile floor. He couldn't tell where his limbs ended and hers began. They untangled, dried off and crawled into bed. His heart swelled with happiness. She was safe and in his arms.

Stone silence in the room seemed like it went on for hours. Her sweet angelic face, void of the smoky eye make-up she wore had been washed away in the shower leaving an innocent girl who didn't know where she was going or what she intended to do once she arrived. Her limited skills consisted of stripping in smoky bars and being pawed all over. Her eyes were open and staring at the ceiling. Maybe she wanted him to speak. This was awkward. What could he say that he hadn't already said?

"I'd like for you to stay with me. If you are uncomfortable we can set you up in a motel in town. Your happiness is important. We can figure it out after we've rested. Let me hold that naked body next to mine and sleep."

Both were breathing evenly within ten minutes.

Chapter 31

Mara threw her arm across the bed and felt the empty space. A glance at the clock beside the bed indicated it was after eleven. The distinct scent of coffee filled the room. She grabbed a robe at the end of the bed, Justin's she assumed, and padded down the stairs. She filled a cup, sipped the dark liquid, and strolled to the French doors that led to the back yard. The sunshine invited her outside.

She took her cup, opened the door and stepped onto the deck. She sat on a wicker love seat, propped her feet up, took in the sweet scent of the pine trees. A couple of Cardinals scrounged for food not far from her. The other two log homes weren't visible from the backyard but she remembered seeing the lights on the porches burning when they got in. The houses looked just alike and were separated by manicured gardens. She hoped she would be here long enough to see them burst into color this spring.

Lost in thought, she failed to hear the front door open. She jumped to her feet, spilling coffee everywhere when the woman spoke.

"I'm sorry. I didn't mean to startle you."

She brushed at the coffee that slowly absorbed into the robe. "That's okay. I get spooked easily."

"Did you get the clothes I sent over this morning? He said you were about my size." She stuck out her hand. "I'm Jamie, by the way, and you must be Mara."

She ran her wet hand down the robe and shook the offered hand. "Yes. Thank you for the loan. I'll make sure they get back to you in good condition."

Jamie waved a hand and sat in a chair across from the love seat. "Don't worry about it. Justin asked me to see that you had everything you need and to show you around."

He had left her alone with people she didn't know. "Where is he?"

"He had business at the bank this morning. He said he would only be a couple of hours. When you're ready I'll take you to meet Ms. Garrett and Amy."

She nodded. "I'd like that. I'll get a quick shower and we can go."

Twenty minutes later the two women entered the log home that sat next to Justin's. The spicy scent of Italian food drifted toward her as soon as they were inside. He stomach growled, and she tried to remember the last time she had eaten. Her hand covered her middle. "Oh my God, something smells wonderful."

Jamie took her arm and pulled her past the elegant great room and into the dining room. A short, stocky woman with beautiful white hair stood in the kitchen. She wore a ruffled apron with red apple print. Mara had only seen one on Father Knows Best reruns. She had to smile at the thought of anyone still having one.

"Mara, this is Ms. Garrett, Justin's mother. We call her Ms. G."

The older woman wiped her hands on the apple apron and reached to take her hand. "I'm happy to meet you. I hope you're hungry. I cooked lasagna and an apple pie for lunch."

"I'm starving and it smells wonderful."

Ms. Garrett grabbed potholders and took the casserole out of the oven. "Well then, Jamie, if you'll set the bar, we'll eat lunch." She set everything out and poured three glasses of tea. "Take a seat."

She took her first bite and closed her eyes. Ms. Garrett's lasagna could hold its own against any chef. "I don't believe I have ever tasted lasagna this good. You could sell this to restaurants in Vegas."

Ms. Garrett chuckled. "Thank you, my dear. I think I'll just make it for friends and family. Do you have family in Las Vegas then?"

She sipped her sweet tea to stall while she decided what to say. "I've lived in Las Vegas all my life and have no family. My mother died when I was young and my father, last I heard, was in prison. I'm the product of foster care. A number of them to be exact." Her voice had taken on a resentful tone that she hadn't intended to let escape.

"Foster homes can't all be bad. Some have to be good or they wouldn't have so many," Ms. G said.

God, these people were so naïve, kind, but naïve. "I've always looked older than I really am and that caused problems. The older men and boys in the families thought I was there to be their sex toy. I didn't agree and usually ran away at the first sign of danger."

Ms. Garrett's fork fell from her hand.

She hadn't meant to shock the older woman. "I'm sorry. It wasn't so bad now that I look back." She lied. "I guess I still hold some resentment."

"Where would you live when you ran away?" Ms. Garrett dabbed her mouth with her napkin.

Should she tell them the whole truth? Would it shock them or should she make up a story. No. The truth was always the best when trying to make a fresh start. All they could do was ask her to leave. It wouldn't be the first time.

The front door opened and a tall handsome man came into the dining room, relieving her from answering. He had a striking resemblance to Rex. After hanging his Stetson on a hook by the door, he retrieved a plate from the cabinet and sat next to Ms. Garrett.

"Mara, this is my oldest son, Carson. He and Amy live in the house to the left. Amy is expecting a baby. Carson, this is Mara. Justin brought her from Las Vegas," Ms. Garrett explained.

Carson reached out his hand to shake hers. "It's nice to meet you. Rex has already filled me in."

That couldn't be a good thing. She had to say something to cover the tension running through her. "When is your baby due?"

"Any day. Amy was due last week and is so uncomfortable. Doctor has her confined to bed and I think she's having some contractions. I believe that Carson Wayne, Jr. will be here this week."

"Is she having the baby at home or at the hospital?" she asked

Carson rubbed his cheek. "If we have time to get to the hospital we will. If not, Mrs. James down the road has five children at home and will come help. Amy is a registered nurse and knows pretty much what to expect. The doctor said everything is normal but we've been told the first child is always unpredictable."

Mara and Jamie cleaned the kitchen while Ms. G went to lie down. Carson finished eating and left in his truck.

"Does Carson work outside of the ranch?" She rinsed the lasagna pan and handed it to Jamie.

"He's a Texas Ranger."

She dropped the sponge. "He's really a Texas Ranger? Don't they ride horses everywhere?"

Jamie laughed and put the dried plates away. "He can ride and does if it's needed. But not to work. It's too far. Tell me about you. How did you meet Justin?"

She grinned, remembering their first meeting. "I accosted him in the casino. I told him I had hit a puppy and asked him to see what he could do for it. It was a farce. The people with me kidnapped him and took him to a dog fight to see if he could save Ran's prize animal."

Jamie stopped drying a pan. "Oh, that's wild. Who is Ran?"

"He's the man who rescued me from the strip club."

Jamie dropped the dish towel on the counter. "Wait. You worked in a strip club?"

She sighed. "It's not a profession I'm proud of, but it paid the bills and I refused to have sex with the customers or date any of them. Except Ran, ironically."

"Did he save the dog?"

"He did everything he could with what he had to work with, but the dog was too beat up."

"That's Justin. He's very passionate about helping the defenseless. He has a heart the size of a basketball. Once we accidentally hit a possum. He made us stop. He wrapped him up to bring back to the barn where he fixed his broken leg. He monitored him until he was well enough to go back on the road. But he had to quarantine him first to make sure he didn't carry rabies. He can't stand to see any animal suffer."

They were walking out of the house and Mara mumbled under her breath, "I guess that's why he was dead set on rescuing me."

"Did you say something?"

"I just said how he helped me." They walked up the path to the log home nearest the barn and Jamie knocked, then opened the door. "Amy. You awake?"

"I'm in the den. Come on in."

Sitting in a recliner sorting baby clothes was an exact duplicate of Jamie. She was just as striking, even with her oversized belly.

"Mara this is the very pregnant Amy. Amy, I want you to meet Mara, Justin's new friend. I'm showing Mara the ranch so we're going to let you rest if you don't need anything."

"No. I'm fine. You two go on and have fun. I'll see you a little later."

Jamie led her toward the barn to a pen with goats inside. They all looked like babies to her.

"Oh how cute. They're so tiny," she exclaimed.

"They're pygmies and can be mean if threatened but most of the time they're sweet. There are more goats on the back part of the property that produce milk."

"I was under the impression this was a horse ranch."

"It is. We inherited the other animals and we're using them to cut the grass in the back pasture, supply fresh milk and butter. I'm going to try my hand at making cheese this afternoon. Would you like to help?"

"I would love to. When can we get started?"

Jamie checked her watch. "Trish, that's my daughter, won't be home for a couple of hours. We can start now. It takes a lot of time and we may have to finish up tomorrow morning."

She leaned on the fence. The goats played and butted heads. They were a joy to watch. "That little guy is trying to suck on one of the other mothers and she won't let him."

Jamie opened the gate and stepped inside. She grabbed the bucket hanging next to the gate and the pygmies came running. Mara stepped back behind the gate.

Jamie glanced over her shoulder. "They won't hurt you. Come on in."

She eased inside slowly. The baby approached and sniffed her hand. He snuggled up to her and baaed. She knelt and the goat climbed on her lap. She stroked the infant and giggled.

Chapter 32

Justin returned to an empty house, unmade bed, and leftover black coffee in the pot. He set his new loan papers on the desk and walked over to his mom's.

"Anyone home?"

"I'm in the kitchen," his mother yelled.

He entered the dining room and walked around the bar where his mom stood in front of her stove. He kissed her on the cheek and poured a glass of tea. "There is a distinct smell of your famous apple pie lingering in the air." He lifted the lid on top of the counter to find a partially eaten apple pie. "It's still the best."

"Thank you, son. Your girlfriend is at Jamie's. They are attempting to make goat cheese. I don't know why. None of us like goat cheese. Too much work and not enough benefit if you ask me."

"Did they say how long they would be?" He spooned a large chunk of pie and ice cream in his mouth.

"They've been gone most of the afternoon. Trish came in, and she hauled butt home as soon as she found out they had company. I haven't heard from them. I don't know if Jamie is cooking tonight or she expects me to. So I whipped up a little something, just in case."

She had fried a couple of chickens so far, a pot of campfire beans sat on the stove and a large bowl of potato salad was in the refrigerator when he opened the door for a glass of milk. He bet, if he looked hard enough, he'd find a cookie sheet with fresh rolls. His mother didn't know how to fix sandwiches. All of her meals were "full meal deals".

"Has Carson come in yet?"

"No. He called to check on Amy and said he would be in late. This is about done. Do you want to call the girls or go get them?"

He finished his pie and washed his dish, then plopped his hat on his head. "I'll ride up and bring them back. I could use some fresh air. I've got some exciting news to tell the family this evening."

"Check on Amy when you go by."

"Yes, ma'am." Justin left the house and walked toward Amy and Carson's. He heard a loud scream and broke into a run. He burst through the front door.

Amy lay on the kitchen floor in a fetal position. Blood pooled under her. He lifted her from the floor and laid her on the couch. He retrieved towels from the bathroom and wrapped her in them, putting a blanket on top to keep her warm. He punched in Carson's number.

"It's time for you to come home." Justin put the phone on speaker and held it close to Amy.

Carson's voice went up an octave. "Can you get her to the hospital or call an ambulance?"

"NO," Amy screamed. "It's too late. Call Mrs. James."

"I can do that, but I'll call Mara and Jamie for back-up," Justin said.

He had to move the phone away when Carson screamed, "Mara? What the hell does a stripper know about delivering babies? Call Mrs. James."

He handed Amy his phone and took hers. He found Mrs. James' number while Amy soothed his hysterical brother. A man answered.

"Sara had an emergency in Dallas and won't be back until tomorrow. I'm sorry. Can you get her to the hospital?" Cold chills ran over him when Mr. James gave him the news.

He hung up and dialed 9-1-1, ordered an ambulance then took his phone from Amy.

"She's out of town. I'm a doctor and Amy's a nurse. With Mara and Jamie to help I'm sure everything will be fine."

"Shit," Carson cursed. Siren blared through the phone as he disconnected.

"Justin there's no time. My water broke and I can feel the baby crowning. You have to call Jamie."

He nodded just as another severe pain hit her. She tightened her grip and screamed, "Get Jamie, now."

He punched in Jamie's number.

"Hi, Uncle Justin. We went to the zoo today at school. I saw the elephants and giraffes and tigers and—"

"Trish, Trish. Listen to me, sweetie. I need to talk to Mommy. It's an emergency."

His niece yelled, "Mommy, it's a 'mergency."

Jamie answered.

"Amy's in labor. We can't get her to the hospital in time and Mrs. James is out of town. She wants you and Mara. Get down here as quick as you can."

"We're on our way."

He threw the phone down. "What can I do, Amy?"

"Hold my hand. I think I'm about to have another one." Her breathing came in short pants as she endured the next contraction.

He had never been around a woman about to deliver a baby before. Puppies, yes, but things weren't going like puppy deliveries. He had no clue what to do but hold her hand. She squeezed his hand so hard, he was sure all the circulation had disappeared.

Jamie, Mara, and Trish, rushed through the front door. The fear reflected in both women's eyes.

The pain subsided and Amy started giving orders. "Send Trish to Nana's. In the bedroom is a container with a blue lid that Mrs. James packed in case of a home delivery. The baby clothes and blankets are in my suitcase next…oh no. Not again."

Justin disappeared and returned a few seconds later with all the supplies. After everyone washed their hands they slipped into the rubber gloves he found in the container. He glanced at Mara. Her face had no color. "Don't cave on me now."

She held Amy's hand until the pain went away. "Amy, tell me if I do anything I shouldn't. I'm probably as scared as you." She looked at him kneeling in front of Amy. "Wouldn't she be more comfortable in bed?"

Amy gave her a weak smile. "There's no time. I'm okay here. I've been assured everything is normal and I'll have a natural birth." She gripped Mara's arm. "I need to push."

"Jamie get the sheets down, bring the water and lay out the instruments," Justin ordered. "He's coming."

With one more push, Carson Junior came into the world, screaming his lungs out. His uncle looked at the tiny person in awe. He wrapped the baby in his little blanket and laid him on his mother's chest. He stopped crying. When Justin looked up at Mara, he saw a tear escape. "He's beautiful, Amy," she caressed the little one's cheek.

Justin cut the cord and laid the new born on his mother's chest. The front door swung open and hit the wall with a thud.

"Amy." Rex rushed into the living room.

"Come meet your son," Amy yelled.

Carson eased closer as if afraid he would disturb the infant. Justin took the baby from Amy and handed him to his dad. He stared down at the tiny pink face. Carson Junior started screaming.

Carson's brows creased and he looked pleadingly at Amy. "What did I do?"

"Let me get him cleaned up and he'll be just fine. Will you help me, Mara?" Justin took the infant and they went into the kitchen. Mara picked up the plastic baby tub sitting on the floor and wrestled it into the sink.

"Clean it out with hot water first then fill it with warm water. Then put several towels on the counter for the baby," he instructed.

She ran hot water in the tub and dumped it several time before filling it with warm water. She folded the towels on the counter.

He laid the baby down and uncovered him. Taking a soft cloth, he wiped the infant down, who screamed during the entire process.

After the baby had been bathed, Justin shooed everyone but Jamie out of the room. "You help her get cleaned up and I'll take care of the rest of this." Once it was done, they helped Amy into the bedroom downstairs. He placed the sleeping little boy in the bassinet next to the bed.

"You rest for a couple of hours before you see people. Junior here will probably be hungry by then," He wrapped the baby blanket tight around the infant and put a cap on his head.

Amy reached out and grabbed his arm. "I can't thank you enough. From puppies to babies. You have a future in the medical field."

He chuckled, his heart skipping a beat. "I think I'll stick to animals."

He left the room and closed the door. "Wow. I'll never get over the miracle of birth." Every muscle in his body ached from the tension.

Carson sat in the living room chair with his elbows on his knees and his head in his hands. He stood as soon as he heard his brother. "Is Amy okay?"

Justin flopped down on the couch. "She's resting. She'll need to see her OB as soon as she feels up to it. Junior needs to be checked out by a pediatrician just to make sure he's good and healthy. Doctor's orders."

"Carson Wayne Garrett, Junior," Carson said in wonder.

Chapter 33

Justin loaded the food his mom had cooked in the golf cart and they road across the drive to Carson and Amy's house. As soon as he entered his phone started ringing. "Here, take this." He handed the pots to Jamie and retrieved his phone. Rex's name appeared on the front screen.

"We have a new baby," he blurted.

"Really? Everything go all right?" Rex asked.

He poured a glass of tea. "It went well. Mara and Jamie did an awesome job helping."

"Mara? What does she know about delivering a baby? Where is Mrs. James?"

"Mrs. James was out of town and the little guy wouldn't wait for an ambulance. Jamie and

Mara assisted me in the delivery. Everyone is here to see him. How's the investigation going?"

"That's what I called about. We still haven't found Dagger. All of our sources are tight lipped or they don't know anything. He's just disappeared. Mara has to come back for the Grand Jury hearing, she's being subpoenaed. It's scheduled for Tuesday. Get Thomas to bring her in the jet and when it's over I'll come back with her."

He let out a heavy sigh and stepped out the back door onto the deck. "Tuesday? She's afraid to go back. There are still too many bikers on the loose."

"Tell her she'll be in a secluded location and have two agents with her at all time."

"Because that worked out so well the last time." Justin vented and ran his hand across his face. "Rex, we just got home and haven't even had time to rest. I'm coming with her."

After a long pause, Rex spoke. "I don't think that's a good idea. You're a distraction to her and trouble tends to follow you."

He stood his ground. "I'm coming."

Rex was silent for a long time. "Have you talked to the rest of the family about your clinic yet?"

"I'm telling them tonight. I'm using an acre, and the money is not coming out of the ranch. It's a done deal, Rex."

"You know I'll help any way I can if you need me."

After they hung up, he helped Mara and Jamie set the table. Ms. Garrett busied herself warming the cooled beans and setting the fruit salad and fresh rolls out. They all gathered around the dining table to eat.

With the dishes done and everyone preparing to depart, he couldn't wait any longer. He shoved his shaky hands in the pockets of his jeans. "I'd like to make an announcement."

Carson cut him off. "You're getting married."

Blood rushed into his face and he glanced at Mara who was turning crimson. "No. I've done all the paperwork at the bank and hired an architect to design Garret Veterinary Clinic. It's going to be a small animal clinic."

His mom jumped up and hugged him. "Oh, son. I'm so happy for you."

He nodded. "I'm planning a large facility because I want it to be a hospital for injured or abused animals."

"That's a pretty tall order, bro. You're going to need help." Carson had the baby in his arms and couldn't get up.

He ran a hand through his hair. "I know. That's why I want to talk to the facility in Las Vegas where I helped out. Mara and I will be going back tomorrow." He looked at her.

She raised her head sharply and her lips pinched together. Her brow raised and her eyes grew wide. "The FBI needs you to testify on Tuesday. We'll leave to come home as soon as that's done."

Her hands clinched the baby's blanket she was folding and she lowered her head. She rose. "If you all will excuse me, it's been a very eventful day. I think I'll go take a shower and go to bed. Call me if you need anything, Amy."

"Nite, Thanks again." Amy took her hand as she passed. Mara nodded.

After she left Carson stood to put his new baby to bed. "I think you upset her."

"Mom, if you're ready, I'll see you home," he grabbed the dishes packed up from dinner and started for the door.

He made sure his mother made it inside safely and then he walked home. "Mara." She didn't answer. He climbed the stairs and heard the shower running. He stripped, walked into the bathroom, and opened the shower door. She stood at one end with her forehead against the tile wall, crying. Stepping inside, he wrapped his arms around her and she leaned her back against him.

"They're going to kill me. I've been on the ranch one day and I know I will love it. I don't want to go back to Vegas."

He held her until she stopped crying. "Nothing will happen to you. I'll be there with Rex along with other agents. They are placing us in an undisclosed location and escorting us to the courthouse. The minute your testimony is over, we will be rushed back to the jet and out of there."

She raised her head and drilled her sky blue eyes into him. "You're going?"

He smiled down at her. "I wouldn't miss it."

They dried off and curled up together in bed. He thought she had fallen asleep and had almost dozed when she spoke. "Are you really opening a clinic?"

"Yep. I went to the bank and got an interim loan. I'll use my trust fund to help buy equipment. I was kind of hoping you would volunteer to help."

She sat up and looked down at him. Her eyes rounded and glowed in the soft light coming from the lamp beside the bed. "You want me? I have no experience. But I could learn with your help."

"I'll teach you. We can do a lot of good. You might even want to take some classes at the college in Tyler."

Her shoulders slumped forward and she hung her head. "I can't go to college. I didn't finish high school."

He couldn't help but care for this woman who had been through so much in her life and survived. He would never know the sorrow and loneliness she must have felt. He vowed to help her find closure and peace so she would be happy. "Don't be so hard on yourself. I've seen you in action. You saved me when I thought I was a goner. You did what you had to in order to pacify Ran and Dagger. You helped deliver my nephew. You can accomplish anything you want. There are ways to get you in college and we'll find them. I'll help."

***

Mara flipped over to get the beam of light coming through the opening in the drapes out of her face. She opened her eyes to find an empty bed. "Justin." He didn't answer.

She slipped into the robe Jamie had brought her and stepped out of the bedroom in time to see him coming up the stairs with a tray that smelled heavenly.

"Damn. You spoiled my surprise. I wanted to bring you breakfast in bed and wake you."

She grinned. "Pretend I'm still asleep." She dropped the robe and sailed through the air, bouncing onto the bed.

He laughed so hard he almost dropped the tray. He set it on the bed and she grabbed a piece of toast. "Umm. Thank you." She leaned over and pecked him on the cheek.

"As much as I would like to join you, I have to meet the architect at the site so he can get started while we're gone. Get a shower and pack and we'll leave as soon as I get back." He kissed her forehead and left her to finish breakfast.

***

Once downstairs, he placed a call to one of his college roommates who had started a private investigation service. After explaining what he wanted, He left the house.

A red pick-up with 'Brian Johnson, Architect,' written on the side waited at the gate when he arrived. He dismantled the alarm and Brian drove through and followed Justin to the spot where the clinic would be built. He told him exactly what he envisioned and Brian made copious notes and a few suggestions.

The two men completed their business and Justin gave him the code to get in the gate and drove back to the house. A chill ran down his back when he noticed the Jeep missing. He hadn't seen it at Carson's or his mom's when he passed. He called Amy anyway.

A crying baby greeted him when she answered. "How's the baby?"

"Hungry. He didn't like the bath. I guess I should have fed him first. Looks like I have a lot to learn." She chuckled.

"You'll do fine. I won't keep you. I just wanted to ask if Mara has been there."

"No. I haven't seen her today. Why? Is something wrong?"

He didn't want to set off alarms. "No. She may have run to the store for something." Mara didn't know the codes to the gate and she would have had to pass him on the drive out.

Maybe she took the road leading up the mountain. He called Jamie and didn't get an answer. Shifting into reverse he backed out, spewing gravel. He took the road around the barn and drove toward Rex and Jamie's on the side of the mountain. He took the curves faster than he should have, but he had to find her.

He cleared the trees and spotted the missing vehicle at the edge of the mountain. She sat on the ground with her knees pulled up to her chest and her arms wrapped around them. He parked next to the Jeep, got out and walked over behind her. She stared straight ahead and her shoulders jerked from her sobs. He sat beside her and respected her silence.

"How did you find me?"

He smiled. "You didn't pass me at the entrance so it was a matter of deduction."

She stared at the beautiful valley below. They were quiet for what seemed like hours to him when she spoke, "Don't make me go."

Her voice was almost a whisper and his stomach dropped. He wanted to take her in his arms and wipe away her fears. She deserved a life free of her past; free from people who used her and preyed upon her. The only way for that to happen was to put the people who abused her behind bars.

"I won't make you do anything you don't want to do. You have survived a lot of pain and misery. Parents who deserted you when you needed them most; living on the streets and surviving; taking your future in your own hands and making a living; dealing with other villains and making the best of it. You went against people who could kill you if you crossed them. You are tougher than you think. Your commitment to life is strong and you will succeed in spite of your own doubts. You've never had anyone who believed in you the way I do. I want to see all of your dreams come true. I want to see you happy and I intend to do everything in my power to make that happen. No, sweetheart, you don't have to testify if you don't want to."

She was silent again and stared into the distance. "Did you take psychology in college?"

He laughed. "No. Why?"

She threw her arms around him and lay her head on his shoulder. "You have such a way with words. What time do we leave?"

Chapter 34

The Cessna landed in Las Vegas as the sun began to set. Rex met them at the tarmac, shook Justin's hand and hugged her. "Let's get going. I think you'll like your temporary home but you won't be here long enough to enjoy it too much."

He led them to a black GMC with dark tinted windows.

Rex got behind the wheel. "The windows are bullet-proof glass. The agency has gone above and beyond to see to your safety." He pointed out the front window at a car exactly like the one they were in. "That car is a decoy. There are two more behind us. We all are going to turn off and go in different directions so if we're being followed, the bad guys won't know which car you're in."

"I'm impressed. But have you caught Dagger?" she asked.

Rex looked in the rearview mirror at her and shook his head. "We think he's left Nevada. He hasn't been spotted."

Justin took her hand. "When will she have to testify at the Grand Jury?"

"Tomorrow morning at ten. As soon as she testifies, you can leave."

He heard the sigh of relief next to him. They traveled through the strip on their way out of the city. Rex turned off the main road and drove into a community with a guard house. He spoke to the guard briefly and the barrier opened for them to enter the subdivision. They took a left on Tomeans Lane then into a gated drive. He stopped, keyed in a code and drove down the palm-lined driveway. At the far end a fountain shot water ten feet into the air. The lights were on in the large Spanish-style house. It looked inviting, almost festive.

"Who lives here?" She stared at the stately mansion.

Rex laid his arm on the back seat and looked at the pair. "No one. It's for sale and is owned by the father of one of the guys in the agency. No one will suspect we would hide you here. There are ten bedrooms, twelve bathrooms, pool, tennis court, and a shooting range. Agents are posted all over the property as well as inside. There is a state-of-the-art security system and guard dogs. You'll be safe here."

"You don't know what those bikers are capable of," she said quietly.

"I guarantee your safety. I'm that confident. I'll be staying here along with the other agents. There are eight on the property. One of the agents will be in charge of monitoring the security cameras all over the property. You're safer here than you would be at a maximum security prison."

"That's a good example. Makes me feel like a prisoner."

Justin stroked her hand. "You're not and you never will be again. Can we go in now? I'm starving and I'm sure Mara is, too."

"All I want is a shower and a bed." She squeezed his hand. "I haven't had a lot of sleep in the past forty-eight hours."

The beige and gold living room greeted them as they entered. Beyond the living room sat a dining area that opened up to a spacious kitchen. The dining table was large enough to seat twenty guests. Mara took it all in.

"This is beautiful. So tastefully decorated. I love it." Entering the kitchen, she opened the refrigerator and found it stocked. "How about a Spanish omelet, bacon, toast, and orange juice?"

Justin's stomach growled. "Sounds good. What can I do?"

"I'm going to look through the rest of the house and check in with the agent covering the security cameras. When will it be ready?" Rex asked from the door.

"About twenty minutes." She yelled over her shoulder as she pulled ingredients from the refrigerator.

He chopped vegetables and grated cheese. She whipped the eggs and put the bacon on to cook. Within twenty minutes the huge omelet was cut into thirds and set on the table with glasses of juice. Rex showed up just in time to eat.

"Did you get anything started on the clinic?" Rex asked his brother.

Justin finished his bite of omelet and wiped his mouth. "The design might be finished when we get back."

"Did you tell the others?"

"Of course. The night the baby was born. I told you that Mara and Jamie helped me deliver him, didn't I?"

"I think you mentioned it. How'd that go?"

"Perfect. When I called Amy earlier, I could hear him screaming in the background. He was hungry. Another Garrett for sure. Trish thinks he's the cat's meow. She's ready for him to go riding with her."

"Well, that will be a while."

"Don't be too sure. Dad had me on a horse at six months. Remember?"

"Dad and Carson are different. I think Carson will be more protective. It won't be long though."

They finished the meal and Justin and Rex discussed the future clinic. He noticed her eyes drooping. "Are you ready for that shower and bed?"

She nodded. He led her up the stairs and yelled over the baluster to Rex. "Any particular bedroom we need to use?"

Rex looked up at them. "Take your pick. The master is at the end of the hall on the right. See you guys in the morning."

Justin opened the door to the master suite and the light came on. Sheers hung from a four-poster bed that had a white fluffy comforter brushing the carpet. She ran her fingers across the bed and strolled to the fireplace.

"Let's light the fireplace."

He grinned. "We might have to adjust the thermostat. It's already warm in here."

She relaxed in one of the chairs in front of the fireplace. "Now if we had a bottle of wine, we'd be set."

He adjusted the thermostat and then flipped a switch. A roaring fire blazed to life. There was a knock at the door. The couple exchanged glances.

"Who is it?"

"Agent Sikes. I have your luggage."

Justin opened the door and helped the agent with the two bags.

"I thought maybe y'all might enjoy this." He grinned and produced a bottle of pinot grigio and two glasses. "We found the wine cellar."

She smiled and took the bottle and glasses. "We were just thinking about looking for a good drink."

"If you need anything Rex is right down the hall." Sikes left, closing the door behind him.

She opened the wine and poured. He took the offered glass and clinked hers. "This is to a successful trip."

She propped her feet up and enjoyed the delicate liquid. "I suddenly have a craving for strawberries."

He laughed and choked on his sip of wine. "We ate and you're still hungry?"

She flashed her beautiful eyes at him and grinned. "Maybe not for strawberries."

He set his glass down, stood and took her glass, setting it beside his. Leaning over he kissed her. She tasted like the pinot. He wanted to devour her mouth. His tongue played with hers. She wrapped her arms around his neck and he put his arm under her legs and carried her to the bed. He laid her down gently and fell next to her. He kissed her lips and explored the inside of her mouth. She followed his lead and tangled her tongue with his. Before long he had removed her clothes and his own. He trailed kisses down her neck to her breasts and played there until the nipples stood at attention. He moved lower to her smooth tummy and nipped around her belly button. He could hear her moans as she arched her hips to his touch. When he reached her most sensitive area he found her moist and inviting.

His discomfort was about to get the best of him but he wanted to take her as high as he could so he continued and slipped his tongue and a finger inside her. She groaned and threaded her fingers through his hair. Her breathing came in short gasps. He wanted them to come together. He positioned himself and slipped inside her. She started the rhythm before he could. She wanted it fast and hard. Not what he had it mind but it would work. He picked up his pace and by the time they fell over the edge of the cliff in complete satisfaction, they were sweating profusely.

He collapsed on top of her and she clung to him like he was her lifeline. Her heart pounded against his chest. He found it hard to get his breathing back to normal. Finally he eased to one side and propped his head in his hand and stared at her. Her eyes closed, and she had a smile on her lips. He leaned over and kissed her. "I sure hope you enjoyed that as much as I did. I've never had sex that great before."

"I've never had sex where I reached a climax before you came along. I didn't think I could."

He kissed her cheek. "There is a big difference in having sex and making love. It has more meaning, more intensity, more love, more feeling on both sides."

Her blue eyes sparkled. "I don't ever want to have just sex again. It will have to be love or it will never happen."

He took her in his arms. "That's my girl."

Chapter 35

A light knock on the door woke him. He walked across the room naked and jerked the door open. "What?"

Rex looked him up and down and grinned. "Have a rough night? Time to get up. We have to be at court in a couple of hours. The DA wants to go over Mara's testimony first."

"Oh, God." Justin heard from behind him. He saw her cover her head.

Rex cocked his head and looked around him. "You will be escorted in the underground entrance by deputies and agents. They're going to take you to one of the conference rooms where you'll meet the DA. After that you'll be taken to the judge's chambers and will stay until they call you to testify. Once you've testified you'll be out of here, taken back to the house to gather your things and put back on the plane. They picked up Dagger in New Mexico."

She raised her head out of the covers and stared at him. "They've all been caught?"

Rex shrugged. "A few lightweights got away into Mexico we think. We'll get them eventually. The law is patient and has a long memory."

She threw the covers off her naked body, grabbed her suitcase, and headed to the bathroom.

Rex raised his brows and looked at Justin. "That went pretty well, don't you think?"

Justin ran his hand through his hair. "Might take a while to get the stripper career out of her. See you downstairs in half an hour." He closed the door and waited for her to get out of the bathroom so he could get in.

His feelings for her had changed. Grown stronger. He didn't know what she intended to do when this was over, but he hoped she would come back with him. She had nothing left in Vegas. He didn't want her to fall back in with the same people. She might go to her friends at the strip club. He didn't want his wife in that business. Wife? Where'd that come from? Did he love her enough to marry her? Yes. Oh yes he did. "I love her. She's my soulmate." But she might have other plans. He would play it by ear and drop a few hints. See how she reacted to the idea.

She came out of the shower with a towel wrapped around her head and nothing else. She looked so inviting he wanted to throw her on the bed and make mad, passionate love to her. She must have read his mind.

"Don't get any ideas. We don't have time. Get a shower and let's get this over with. I want to go by, see Dixie and sell her the Harley. That will give me a little cash and I have a few things in a safety deposit box I need to pick up at the bank. The money from the Harley should be enough to get me by until I can go to work at the clinic with you."

He headed to the bathroom and stopped at the door. What did she say? She wanted to work at the clinic? His heart bounced in his chest. He wanted to pick her up and swing her around. He put that on his 'to do list' for later.

After they were dressed, they walked together down to the main floor. Rex stood by the front door with four men in black suits. Four identical vehicles sat in the circular drive with the engines running. Justin helped her into the third car in line and slipped in beside her. The cars drove the long driveway and each went in a different direction. He took her shaking hand and ran his thumb over the top. She gave him a fake smile and turned back to the window.

Her body stiffened against him when two motorcycles drove alongside of the black car at a red light.

"Rex said the bikers who are not in jail have all disappeared." Justin reminded her.

She relaxed her grip on his hand and stopped shaking. She looked at him and nodded.

When they arrived at the courthouse the driver pulled around back drove into an underground parking garage designated for judges and deputies with prisoners. The suits opened their doors and checked the area before opening the back door. They were led into the building. They were taken to a small conference room. An agent sat with them and one stood guard at the door. Eventually a tall redheaded woman bustled in with a large stack of files. "I'm DA Kennedy. I'll be presenting this case to the grand jury personally. If we could just go over your testimony and then I'll answer any questions you have."

For the next hour Mara told her story with Ms. Kennedy asking questions and taking notes. She had a remarkably good memory for details. As the time grew closer to present her case, the DA thanked her, told her she would see her in the grand jury room, and left.

They were placed in one of the judge's chambers. A suit sat with them and one stood guard at the door.

She paced. He followed her movements. He wished he could do something to help her.

A deputy brought two Cokes and a thermos of coffee. "It shouldn't be long. You might need something to drink. Sorry, I guess alcohol is not allowed in the courthouse." He chuckled and set the drinks on the table.

Time stood still. He kept looking at the clock and finding ten minutes had passed since the last time he looked. Finally, the door swung open and two deputies and Rex stepped inside.

"They're ready for you, Mara."

After a quick glance at Justin, she followed Rex out of the room. He wasn't allowed in the courtroom in case they needed him to testify as well. All he could do at this point was wait and check the time. Ten minutes, twenty minutes, but when the clock hit sixty minutes, he began to worry. He opened the door and spoke to the deputy posted outside.

"Do you have any idea how much longer they're going to keep her?"

The deputy shook his head. "No. Sometimes these things go on for hours. It's the nature of the beast."

The news didn't make him feel any better.

Twenty minutes later a deputy came for him, escorting him back to the judge's chamber that she would be brought to when she finished testifying. After what seemed like another hour, she came into the judge's chambers. Her face was splotched from crying and her eyes were red. He took her in his arms and held her until Rex interrupted.

"It time to go, you two."

After settling in the car, she tapped Rex on the shoulder. "I have some business I need to take care of before we leave Las Vegas. Do you think it would be possible for Justin to take me out for an hour or so?"

Rex glanced at the driver then back at her. "That's not a good idea. The only way I'll agree is if you take Agent Statler with you. He'll take you wherever you want to go. You never know what kind of connections De Luca has or if he'll use them from jail. We didn't protect you this far to have something happen now. Do you think you can wrap things up today so we can leave or do we need to wait until tomorrow? I need to let Jamie know when I'll be home."

Justin glanced at his watch. It was already two in the afternoon. "Let's plan to leave tomorrow."

She smiled. Her eyes twinkled with excitement after the conversation. As soon as they arrived at the safe house, she changed into her leather pants and tank top and rushed downstairs to join Justin.

The first stop was The Pink Titty. Dixie was coming off the stage when she spotted Mara. She rushed toward them and wrapped her arms around her.

"Dixie, you're choking me."

The older woman released her and looked at Justin. "Well you sure look better than you did the last time I saw you." She grinned. "Y'all come on back so we can talk. What are you doing here? Oh, and who is this tall drink of water?" She batted her eyes at Statler, who seemed completely nonplussed by the naked women on the stage and oblivious to Dixie's flirtations.

Dixie led them back to a fairly normal looking break room. Or it would have been if there hadn't been half a dozen half-dressed women lounging around reading the paper, smoking, or painting their nails. The threesome sat around a small dining table while Statler stood guard at the door, arms crossed over his huge chest. Dixie made coffee in an ancient machine. Once she had them served, she sat next to Mara.

"Now tell me everything. Ran has been all over the news, racketeering, murder, sex-trafficking! I tell you I knew he was a bad apple but I had no idea how bad or I would never have let you go with him. You seemed to have landed on your feet though."

"I'm leaving town for good and I want to sell you the Harley if you want it."

Dixie spewed coffee and her eyes grew wide. "You want to let me buy your Harley? Oh Mara, are you sure? That's your baby."

"I'm sure. I have no need for it and I need the money."

They agreed on a price and Dixie left. She returned a short time later and handed her five thousand one hundred dollar bills. Mara pulled the title from her purse and signed it over.

Dixie brought her up to date on all the latest gossip and they laughed about her latest nursing course. Seems she was having trouble with sex education.

After Justin and Mara left the strip club they drove to the bank.

"I won't be a minute." She reached for the door handle.

Justin started to protest but the agent did it for him.

"Sorry, ma'am. Where you go, I go." Statler opened the door for her.

After a lengthy debate, they agreed to let her go into the cubical where she opened her safety deposit box alone. She came out a few minutes later with an overstuffed bank bag. They climbed into the car and she threw the bag on the seat beside her.

"I guess I've done everything I need to do. The FBI said I can't take anything out of the house so I'll have to buy a new wardrobe. I don't think what I had will fit in at the ranch anyway."

"Then let's go shopping," he suggested.

She grabbed his arm, eyes wide. "Can we?"

"Let me run by the animal clinic I worked with for a few minutes to ask Doctor Tam a few questions and we'll shop. I do have a question for you though."

Concern etched across her face. Her smile turned to a frown. "Hit me with it."

"Did you mean what you said back there about working with me?"

"You offered it to me. If you don't want me to, I'll find something else." She turned her head toward the front.

He put his hand on her cheek and turned her to face him. "That's not what I meant. I do want you to help me. As a matter of fact I'm ecstatic about it."

"Oh good. You haven't changed your mind."

"Not on your life. There is another thing. You said the other night that you loved me. Was that heat of passion or are you really in love with me?"

"I have fallen in love with you big time. But I'm a little reluctant to say it again in case you don't have the same feelings," she glanced shyly at Statler who waited patiently for directions to the next place they were going and doing an excellent job of pretending not to hear them.

"I've dated a few women in my life and not one could make me feel the way you do. I realized this morning I love you with everything that is in me. So do you think we should do something about it?"

She looked at him, frowned, and cocked her head. It dawned on her what he meant. "I think that would be the proper thing to do." Her smile covered her face like a kid going to the fair for the first time.

"Then I know where we're going." He leaned forward and gave Statler the address of their next stop.

Chapter 36

He grinned when he saw Mara and the doc walk into The Pink Titty. He knew she would show up. The suit with them was a fed. You could spot 'em a mile away. He lit a cigarette and waited. They'd be out in a while and he'd pay the legendary Ms. Dixie a visit.

It had taken some clever moves on his part to stay out of the eyes of the law. But he did it. Of course shaving his beard had hurt. He felt like he was giving up his identity. When he borrowed an old friend's truck, he had to leave his bike behind. That was like losing a limb. He'd get it back if he had to resort to deadly force.

An hour later the door opened and the trio stepped out and got into a black GMC. Another indication the FBI had a tight rein on her. The vehicle pulled away and he stepped out of the truck, lowered his cap to hide his eyes, and walked across the street to the strip club.

The bouncer stood inside the door and stopped him. "There's a cover unless you want a private."

He didn't look up. "Private with Dixie in the Blue Room."

The Blue Room was the only private room set off from the others. If this got ugly, no one would hear.

"That'll be three-hundred, in advance." The bouncer held out his hand.

Good, the bouncer didn't recognize him. He dug his wallet out and handed over the cash. The bouncer led him to the back and opened the door.

"I'll get her." He shut the door.

He looked around the familiar room. Nothing had changed. Same color, a sickening blue, same couch with all the stains. He took a position behind the door. It didn't take long and the door opened.

"What the hell? There's no one—"

He pinned her with one arm from behind and covered her mouth with the other. "Hello, Dixie," he whispered close to her ear.

She inhaled, making a humming noise through her nose. Her body stiffened under his hand.

"I'm going to release you, but if you scream or try to escape, you're dead. Do you understand?"

Dixie whimpered and nodded. She fell forward as soon as he removed his hands. "Dagger. I thought they caught you."

He chuckled. "You know me better than that. They have who they think is me."

She eased into a chair. "What do you want? You know I don't make enough to support myself so it can't be money."

He had pulled the switchblade from his boots and pointed it at her. "I do want money, but not yours. It's Ran's."

Dixie frowned at him. "Fuck, Dag. What the hell makes you think I'd have that scumbag's money?"

He gritted his teeth. "I'm not stupid, bitch. I know you don't have it, but Mara does."

"You're wrong."

"She don't know it but she has it. Where is she?"

"How would I know? I ain't seen her."

He backhanded her and knocked her off the chair. She looked up and blood oozed from the corner of her mouth.

"You're lying. I saw her leave a few minutes ago. Tell me where she's going or I'll start cutting pieces out of you."

Dixie wiped her mouth. "She didn't say."

He stabbed the knife into her hand. She screamed. "Where?" He quickly covered her mouth.

She jerked her head to the side. "Okay, okay. She's going to Texas."

He grabbed her other hand. "That's a big state. Where?"

She shook her head. He cut her other hand. "Stop. Tyler. Garrett Quarter Horse Ranch."

"That wasn't so hard, now was it?" Dagger grabbed her hair, pulled her head back and ran the sharp switchblade across her throat. She gasped, grabbed her neck, and fell to the floor. A gurgling noise came from her as she tried to breathe through the blood. Her hand dropped and she no longer moved. He left the room and exited through the side door.

Outside, he opened the glove box and retrieved the phone he had borrowed with the truck. He pulled the map up. The drive would take him twenty-two hours. He could knock off a couple of hours if he had the bike. He checked to see if he had enough Provigil to keep him going. He had three pills. Just enough to get him to Texas

Chapter 37

The plane landed in a pouring rain. The turbulence had been hard on Mara. She had been to the bathroom twice and still felt sick. But she was happier than she had ever been in her life. The handsome cowboy vet sitting next to her had given her everything she ever dreamed of but never imagined happening.

They stepped off the plane and into one of the farm trucks. Thomas drove them to Carson and Amy's. She insisted on seeing the baby before going home.

The little guy was asleep when they arrived and she refused to let Amy wake him. The contentment on his face let her know he would be a sassy, spoiled little boy. She intended to see to it and become friends with Trish. She loved kids and wanted a dozen of her own. But if it didn't happen she would settle for loving the animals.

Justin stepped up behind her and slipped an arm around her waist. He whispered in her ear. "Let's call a family meeting at Mom's." She nodded but let him do the talking.

"I need y'all to come over to Mom's in about an hour. We have a big surprise for everyone."

"You're having a baby," Carson blurted out.

"No. Come over and find out."

The rain had stopped so he took her hand and they walked to his mom's house. His mother sat at the counter working a puzzle and looked up when they entered.

"You're back. If I'd known you were coming I would have cooked." The older woman got up, went around the counter, and opened the refrigerator.

"We aren't hungry, Mom. The rest of the family are coming over. We have a surprise."

The door opened a while later and the house filled with chatter. Amy sat the baby's carrier on the counter. He had slept through the trip and being jostled around.

Everyone settled around the bar. Ms. Garrett came around the counter, pulled the baby's blanket down, and kissed his chubby cheek. "There's Nana's baby. I haven't seen you all day." She hugged Trish. "Or you either. You don't come to see me since moving up the mountain."

"Mommy won't let me ride Buttermilk by myself." Trish puckered her lower lip.

"We'll work on that when you get a little bigger." Rex ruffled her hair and sat on a barstool. "What's the big surprise?"

"You have a surprise? Is it for me?" The little blonde jumped up and down, pulling on Justin's pant leg.

He leaned over and picked her up and placed her on a stool next to Rex. "I'll have something for you soon, squirt. This surprise is for Mara and me."

He poured tea for him and Mara and sat at the table since all the chairs at the bar were taken. He took her hand. "You all know I've started the process on the clinic and Mara has agreed to work with me there. She'll hopefully be taking classes at one of the colleges in Tyler.

If she enjoys it, she may go to A&M for more extensive studies."

"That's awesome, Mara. It sounds like something you will be very good at," Amy told her.

"We haven't checked into anything yet. This is something we were discussing before we left Las Vegas. I've explained to her that I want the clinic, besides being a small animal hospital to take in unwanted strays, abused and neglected animals. I want it to run as smoothly as the clinic I worked at in Vegas. When we were there I stopped by the clinic to check on the dogs that were confiscated in the raid. All of the animals that were saved are doing great. That's the kind of clinic I want."

"Seems like a lot of work. How do you plan to take care of all your new customers who bring their animals in for check-ups?" Rex asked.

"With Mara's help, we can do it. I shouldn't have any problems getting certified because of the ranch."

"So it's not for the money but the humanitarian thing. I like it. If you get a big bunch of rescued animals, I think everyone on the ranch will be willing to help out. You've always had a soft heart, bro. I'm proud of you." Rex slapped him on the back.

Carson stood and shook his hand. "If you need any help with financing I'll be happy to help."

Ms. Garrett piped in. "The ranch is doing quite well and a quarter belongs to you. Dip into the funds any time you need it, son."

His grin spread across his face. "I appreciate the generosity but it has been taken care of. I don't need any money. Your support is the most important thing. Thanks guys."

He glanced at Mara. Tears streamed down her cheeks. "Is something wrong?"

She shook her head. "No. I've never been around such a caring family. I'm just happy to be a part of it."

He took her hand. "There is one more thing I need to tell you."

"Oh, good grief. I knew there had to be a catch. Spill it, boy," Carson demanded.

"No catch. It's great news." He looked at her and she smiled. "Mara and I were married in Las Vegas."

Ms. Garrett gulped, jumped up, and hugged Mara.

Jamie grinned and embraced her as well. "Congratulations."

Amy squealed, the baby jumped and started crying. "Yes." She hugged Justin and waited her turn to hug his new wife.

The two brothers pumped his hand until it went numb.

"You know what that means? We have to throw you a reception. We'll invite the neighbors, Carson can grill steaks and Ms. Garrett can supervise Amy's cooking." Jamie beamed.

"Before you start the preparations, Mara and I will be going on a honeymoon. We're going to Houston for a few days. I think she deserves a small vacation." He saw the surprise written on her face.

"You didn't tell me," she laughed.

"I just did."

"When are we leaving?" she asked.

"First thing in the morning."

Jamie stood and took Trish's hand. "Then I suggest you get to bed. I know it's time for this little beauty to go to sleep."

"I'm not ready. I want to talk about the party." Trish tried to keep her eyes open.

Amy took the baby out of his carrier. "This one is ready to eat. Will we see you before you leave?"

He shook his head. "I want to get an early start. You may not be up."

Everyone said their good-byes and he walked Mara home. "Are you upset with me for not telling you?"

She squeezed his hand. "Not really. I'm used to spur of the moment changes. I've never been to Houston. Heck, I've never been anywhere. I think it will be fun."

***

Mara couldn't sleep. She didn't know if the anxiety of the hearing or the excitement over her marriage was to blame. A nagging concern about the future played heavily on her mind. Would she be a good wife? Mother? Did he want children? She hoped so. He wasn't like the others she had known. He loved her like she had never been loved. She could feel it deep down. Her life would be nothing but happy from now on. So why did she have the feeling that something was missing?

Chapter 38

Mara awoke to the smell of coffee brewing. She must have fallen asleep around four. She drug her tired body out of bed and went into the bathroom to get a shower. When she stepped back into the bedroom, Justin had brought her a steaming cup and he was throwing clothes into a suitcase sitting on the bed.

"We won't need much. If we decide to stay longer we can purchase what we need." He stopped his task. "I would like to show you the Gulf."

"I've never seen an ocean."

"Well, this one is dirty. Not clear blue like in Florida. But it still has its own beauty and I want to be the one to share it with you." He crossed the room and kissed her then slapped her lovingly on the butt. "Now get moving."

She had never felt as loved as she did at that moment. She knew she was in love with him before but her heart melted in her chest and flowed through her veins. They were one together.

She made the bed while he carried the bags to the car. His cell, he had left on the night stand buzzed.

"Would you get that, please," he yelled from the bottom of the stairs.

"Hello?"

"This is Thomas. I need to speak to Justin. Is he around?"

"Sure. He just went to put the luggage in the car." She met him coming up the stairs. "It's Thomas."

"What's up?" He paused. "I'll be right there." He looked up the stairs at her. "We've got a mare having a difficult labor. I have to go check her out. It shouldn't take long."

She smiled. "That will give me time to straighten up. Go."

He climbed up and kissed her then rushed out the door. She busied herself picking up their dirty clothes and wet towels. She didn't have much to do. Justin kept a clean house. Two hours passed and he hadn't called or come back. She walked over to Amy's.

Amy opened the door when she knocked. "I hope this isn't a bad time. I just wanted to see how you and the baby are doing."

"Come in. It's never a bad time here on the ranch. I'm about to give him a bath. You want to help?"

"I would love to."

Amy picked the baby up from his carrier and they went into the kitchen. "I have to warn you, he doesn't like baths and will let you know it."

Once the little one was clean, clothed, and fed, he slept. She and Amy sat in the living room drinking iced tea.

"Did you hear about the horse that's having trouble delivering?" She couldn't help but be suspicious since he had been gone so long.

Amy set her glass down. "Carson called a few minutes before you arrived. The foal is refusing to come out and Justin thinks it may be breech."

"It worried me that he hadn't called. We were about to leave when Thomas called."

Amy leaned over and patted her hand. "Sweetie, when you live on a working farm or you're married to a lawman, animals and criminals come first."

She frowned, ashamed of herself for being suspicious. "It could be worse. I could have married a surgeon."

Amy laughed. "You can go up to the barn if you like. They won't mind and it might make you feel better."

The two women visited until the baby woke for his next meal. She strolled into the barn that looked nothing like the one where the dogs had been. She followed the sound of voices coming from one of the stalls. Her new husband had rolled his white shirt sleeves up that was now covered in blood. She propped her arms on top of the gate, it squeaked. He turned around and saw her.

"I'm sorry, baby. I can't leave her like this." He continued his attention back to the horse.

The animal was clearly in distress. She continued to admire her husband's determination to save the foal and its mother. The mare's cries were soothed with his gentle hands and soft voice. How did she get so lucky? She had dreamed of finding a man like him someday but held little hope. She would wait on him as long as he wanted.

The afternoon sun begin to fade. The lights come on in the stall. The three men continued to assist the mare. She walked back to the house and checked the freezer. Justin hadn't eaten all day and would be hungry when he came in.

"Let's see. Something that will warm up well." The freezer contained steaks. A lot of steaks. She found a package of hamburger and decided on Salisbury steak and went to work.

When dinner was done, she ate and fixed Justin's plate. After wrapping plastic over his, she sat at the bar and ate then cleaned the kitchen. She settled on the couch in front of the television.

***

After a grueling day, Justin wanted a shower and his wife curled up next to him in bed. It had been exhausting but he was satisfied the mare and new foal were going to be fine.

He drug his tired limbs into their house. She lay on the couch, sound asleep. He knelt and kissed her. Her hand swung out, hitting him.

"Ouch," he yelled.

"Oh no. I'm so sorry. I guess old instincts are going to take a little time to forget." She wrapped her arms around his neck and kissed his cheek. "How's the mare?"

He briefed her on mare's condition. "She had a beautiful little colt. He looks just like my horse." He covered her hand. "I'm sorry we couldn't leave this morning. We can leave now, if you want."

She stood and pulled him toward the kitchen. "Nope. You're going to eat and get some sleep. I cooked."

He finished the plate she warmed for him and went to get a shower. When he entered the bedroom, Mara pulled the covers back, and he collapsed next to her. They spooned their warm bodies together and fell asleep.

Chapter 39

Dagger had made the trip in record time. He had no trouble locating the ranch and finding a hill were he could see the whole place. The binoculars provided him a close up and he recognized Justin and Rex. When he saw the doctor enter the last house in the circular drive, he knew where to find her. The lights inside went off a short time later and relief washed over him. He could get some much needed sleep until morning and then decide what to do next.

***

They slept late. She wanted to see the foal and went with Justin to check on the animals. The brown and white paint was enjoying his breakfast when they looked over the gate. "He's so cute. Two new babies within three days; that's so neat."

"I think this colt should go to junior since they were born in the same week." He stepped out of the stall after checking momma and baby. Thomas locked the gate behind them. "They're going to be fine. Give them a couple more days in the stall then let them out. If there are any problems while I'm gone, call Doctor Montgomery." Thomas nodded.

They left the ranch for their honeymoon close to noon. He could hardly contain his excitement. He didn't know if he could keep the secret he had. The words rested on his lips, waiting to pop out. He had to bite his tongue several times during the long drive.

***

Three hours later the traffic got heavier and buildings dotted the horizon. It wasn't anything she hadn't seen in Vegas except there were no neon lights. She strained to take in the slums, people and buildings. There didn't seem to be an end to the chaos. The interstate system was a mass of webs, turns and construction everywhere. It amazed her how massive it looked.

"If you didn't have GPS a person could get lost."

He agreed. "You could get lost *with* GPS. Hopefully, we won't."

Her curiosity got the best of her. "Where are we going?"

"It's not much farther. I'm looking for Grayson Road exit. The sign said it's in two miles."

He took the exit and drove away from downtown Houston. Soon they started passing expensive subdivisions. The homes where huge. The lush green landscapes were in direct contrast to the desert around Las Vegas. "I can't believe how beautiful the yards are. It must rain a lot."

"Houston is close enough to the ocean to get its share of rain. It washes away a lot of the smog and dust." He leaned forward. "Here's the subdivision we need."

"Are we going to see someone you know?"

"Indirectly."

What did that mean? Either he knew them or didn't. He was being very secretive and it made her nervous.

Justin took a right into Shady West subdivision, separated from the sounds of heavy traffic by a ten foot brick wall that stretched as far as she could see. The homes were all brick. They were as wide as they were tall and sat back off the street. Some she couldn't even see for the massive trees. The GPS beeped and he took a right, pulling up to an iron gate. He pushed the button on the call box

"May I help you?"

"Justin and Mara Garrett to see Marquita."

The gate buzzed open.

"It's like something out of a dream," she whispered. It had to be the largest home she had ever seen. Her heart hammered against her ribs. She trusted him. So why was she suddenly afraid? As they approached the house she spotted an older woman with beautiful white hair standing on the columned front porch. She could tell by looking at her that she came from money. She wasn't someone who had married into it or inherited it; she grew up living in luxury. She stood straight, head raised, integrity, and confidence written all over her.

He parked and went around to open her door. "Where are we?" Her insides were in thermal. He was being so evasive and that scared the hell out of her. Her hands shook.

"There's someone I want you to meet." He took her hand and helped her out of the car.

The older woman had a wistful smile on her face. She hurried down the steps to the couple. Her eyes bore into Mara, hard. She became uncomfortable under the older woman's scrutiny. Just when she was about to say something, the woman threw her arms around her.

"My baby! You look just like your mother."

She looked over the older woman's shoulder at Justin. He smiled at her, reassuringly. "Mara, this is Marquita Inez Butler."

Her stomach shoved up into her throat cutting off her air. Butler was her mother's maiden name.

"How?" She was at a loss for words.

Mrs. Butler held her at arm's length. "You have her eyes and mouth. I can't believe how much you resemble her. Please come inside. I'll have tea brought to the sitting room and we can talk." She kept an arm around Mara's waist as if afraid she would disappear.

In the foyer, a large painting of her mother hung on the wall. It was an exact replica of a picture she had retrieved from the safety deposit box in Las Vegas. She had been young, maybe in her teens, when the painting was done. Long before the drugs changed her appearance. She gasped and covered her mouth. Her knees buckled. Justin grabbed her before she could hit the floor. She gasped for breath.

"William, please come help," Mrs. Butler called out.

He picked her up and followed Mrs. Butler into a sitting room. A tall man in a black suit provided a cool cloth that he applied to the back of her neck. Her breathing came in short pants.

"Breathe, baby. Look at me. Breathe normally," he told her.

Her heart began to slow and she could breathe. She kept her eyes on him, not daring to look at the older woman.

"Why didn't you tell me?"

"I'm so sorry. I wanted to surprise you. I guess I made a mistake."

Mrs. Butler sat beside her on the sofa. "Don't be hard on him, dear. His intention were good."

She looked at the woman. "Are you really my grandmother?"

"I am. I've been searching for you for a long time. You can only imagine my excitement when the detective Justin hired contacted me." She hugged her again. "Now you're here, and we have a lot of catching up to do." She addressed the man she had summoned. "William, please have Gloria bring tea and some of those little cakes she made."

"Yes, madam." The man disappeared through the large double doors.

Mrs. Butler shifted on the sofa to face her. "Congratulations on your marriage. I think you have picked someone who cares for you deeply. Hang on to him for dear life because his kind are hard to find. Your grandfather has been gone five years and I will never find another one like him."

She found her voice. "How long were you married?"

"Forty-seven wonderful years. I miss him dearly."

They spent several hours talking. She learned that her mother had gotten pregnant and was afraid to tell her parents so she ran off with her father. Her mother's parents were devastated. They hired several different detectives after reporting her missing.

"You didn't kick her out?"

Mrs. Butler's hand flew to chest. "Absolutely not. We would have helped her any way we could. Although, Gerald would have made sure that boy who got her pregnant was no longer in the picture. We didn't like him one bit. That only made your mother want him that much more."

She lowered her head and mumbled, "That would have saved a lot of heartache."

A soft knock came, and the door opened. William entered. "Madam, will you be having dinner this evening?"

She glanced at her Rolex. "Oh my. I'm having so much fun getting caught up with my granddaughter, I forgot about dinner. I bet you two are famished. Let's go into the dining room." Mrs. Butler rose.

The elegant twelve foot mahogany dining table had three place settings. A crystal chandelier glowed warmly above.

"I don't have as many guest as we did when Gerald was alive, but I still insist on the evening meal being special. I hope you enjoy it."

Justin held Mrs. Butler's chair at the head of the table and then helped seat Mara. He sat across from her. The older woman rang a small bell next to her plate and the servants served the first course.

"I don't see how you stay so thin." Mara dug a spoon into the delicate white chocolate dessert that was the last course. She closed her eyes and moaned. Three bites and she had to lay the spoon down. She glanced at Justin. He was watching her.

"I quit two spoons ago." He grinned.

"Let's retire to the study where we can visit before bed time. I want to show you something." Her grandmother rose.

They followed Mrs. Butler through the house to the study. A large wooden desk sat in front of a massive rock fireplace. Above the mantle sat another photo of her mother when she was a child. Mara stared up at the beautiful child in a white frilly dress sitting in a swing attached to a large oak tree. How had her life spiraled out of control? The only thing she could think of was her father's influence. She didn't know much about him except that he had been arrested and convicted of attempted murder, robbery, and distribution of a controlled substance. He had hooked her mother on the drugs that eventually killed her. She would never forgive him for what he did to her mother or her mother for being so weak to allow it. She mourned for the little girl in the picture who had once had the world at her fingertips.

Chapter 40

After Dagger saw the Jeep pull into a driveway, he circled the block. He wasn't worried about the locked gate. He had gotten into more secure places than that. He located a closed shopping center a couple of miles from the house. An overgrown field separated the subdivision from the empty parking lot. He made sure the switchblade was tucked inside his boot before getting out.

He hiked across the field and to a small alley behind the houses. He stayed in the shadow of the tall fences that ran behind the mansions until he reached the back of the house where Mara had gone. He climbed on one of the garbage cans and peeked over the fence. Several trees stood between him and the house. He could hide among them and not be seen. He jumped over, waited in case of dogs, and unlocked the gate. He raced to a large tree to hide until dark.

***

Justin followed the two women. William stood next to the bar, pouring brandy. He brought the tray over, setting it on the desk.

"Will there be anything else, madam?"

"No. Thank you, William." Mrs. Butler picked up one of the leather photo albums off the desk and took it over to the sofa. "Come, sit." She patted the spot next to her.

He took a seat next to the older woman and Mara sat on the opposite side. Mrs. Butler opened the first of many albums and began to take them down memory lane.

"This is Jessica from birth to five." She flipped through the pages, stopping now and then to explain the scene.

Mara sniffled. This had to be trying on her. She had gone from knowing nothing about her family to finding her grandmother. He hoped this would bring her closure and some peace.

They spent the next two hours going through the albums. Mrs. Butler yawned and he knew they needed to leave.

"I think we should be going." He stood.

Mrs. Butler closed the album. "Nonsense. You will stay here. We have four more albums to go through and I'm sure Mara has a lot more questions."

Mara stood beside him. "We don't want to impose."

"Poppycock. There are eight bedrooms in this monstrosity and more bathrooms than that. The housekeeper has prepared the guest suite for you. Besides, I'm not through loving on my only granddaughter." She laid the album on the desk and pushed a buzzer that summoned William. "Please show our guests to their room." She kissed Mara on the cheek and hugged Justin. "You have made my life complete and I'll forever be grateful. I will see you two in the morning."

He wrapped an arm around Mara and followed William up the double, curved stairs to the room assigned them. The fireplace roared and filled the room with warmth. She strolled around, running her fingers over the delicate silk-covered chairs in front of the fireplace to the satin covering on the king-size bed. Double doors opened onto a balcony that overlooked a pool and well-maintained garden.

"I've never seen anything this elegant."

He shed his jacket and laid it across a covered bench at the foot of the bed. "Are you angry with me?"

"I was. Now I'm grateful. You have accomplished something I've wanted and never dreamed it happening. She's exactly like I imagined. Kind, caring, and she loved my mother with all her heart. I'm proud to be her granddaughter. I love you for making my dreams come true."

He hurried across the room and hugged her to him. "I only want you to be happy. I'm glad it turned out this way. Just remember, I love you and you call the shots. We can leave at any time."

"She has so much more to share with me and I have questions. I want to hear it all. I want to know her, to get close to her and be what she lost when my mother left. I am finally home."

He devoured her lips and when their tongues met she started unbuttoning his shirt. It didn't take long for them to both shed their clothes, and he lowered her to the white fur rug in front of the fire. It became an intense need for both of them that left them completely satisfied. They retreated to the bed and slept spooned in each other's arms.

***

The lights upstairs had gone out an hour earlier. Dagger figured they should be sound asleep by now. He crept around the pool, climbed the balcony structure and listened at the doors. He didn't know which of the two bedrooms Mara would be in, so he went for the first on his left. Taking a glass cutter he had picked up years ago, he attached the suction to the glass and made a circle. The round piece of glass popped out. He reached his hand inside, unlocked the door, and waited. No alarm went off.

The dark room provided little light. Once his eyes adjusted to the surroundings, he could see the bed with one person in it. He eased forward, catching his foot on something on the floor. A lamp shattered, startling the sleeping woman. She sat up in bed and screamed. He pounced across the room, slapped his hand across her mouth, and pinned her down.

***

Mara shot straight up in bed. Something had awakened her. She held her breath and listened. Something didn't feel right. She glanced at Justin, who slept soundly. Shoving the cover off, she grabbed her robe, tiptoed out of the bedroom, and walked down the hall to her grandmother's room.

She pressed her ear to the door then knocked softly. "Mrs. Butler, are you all right?"

"Run, Mara," the woman called out behind the door.

She slammed the door open. It banged against the back wall, with a loud thud. Horror engulfed her. Dagger had her grandmother on her knees, holding her head back by her hair, and a knife pressed against her throat.

Don't panic…. "You don't want to hurt her, Dagger. You want me. Take me. Leave her alone."

He laughed a cruel sound. "Sure. And what's to say she don't call the cops as soon as we leave? I don't think so. I don't leave witnesses. You can ask Dixie about that."

"What did you do to Dixie?" Her heart almost stopped.

Mrs. Butler grabbed her chest and her eyes rolled back. She went limp.

"I don't have time for this shit." He threw the unconscious woman to the floor.

Mara screamed and raced across the room to her grandmother.

Dagger had her trapped in his burley arms before she could kneel beside the unconscious woman.

Chapter 41

Justin awoke to a scream. He reached across the bed to find it empty. "Mara," he called and didn't get an answer. He jumped out of bed and threw on his pajama bottoms. Grabbing the gun Rex insisted he bring, he stepped into the hall and looked toward the stairs. At the far end, a soft light appeared in Mrs. Butler's open door.

He rushed toward the door, pressed his back to the wall and took a quick peek in the room. Mrs. Butler lay on the floor. Justin glanced around. When he didn't see anyone, he checked the older woman's pulse. It was steady.

"Mrs. Butler," he said. She didn't answer.

A scraping noise came from the balcony. He moved toward the balcony doors. An intruder was climbing down with a lifeless Mara over his shoulder. Justin rushed to the stairs. He had to find the back door in the massive house.

At the bottom of the stairs, he yelled and prayed the household staff was light sleepers. "William, there's an intruder. Call 9-1-1. Need the police and an ambulance. Mrs. Butler is unconscious." He knocked a vase of flowers off the kitchen island, shattering it on the floor. He called out again before reaching the back door. "William. Call the police."

He saw the man slip into the dense trees beyond the pool. Justin ran harder than he ever had. By the time he reached the fence at the back, the gate stood open. He rushed through and looked up and down the alley. Nothing. A scream came from the field that ran alongside the alley.

"Stop squirming or I'll kill you here."

A man's voice carried through the air. Justin followed the sound.

"Justin." Mara yelled again.

He shoved the tall weeds aside, caught sight of them, and pointed the gun. "Drop her or I'll shoot."

Dagger pulled her in front of him. "Back off Garrett or I'll kill her."

The moon cast a reflection on the knife the biker held to her throat. Justin didn't want to risk hitting Mara.

"Let her go, Dagger. You don't need her. Take me."

He backed up using her as a shield. "You don't have the bank account number. She does."

"No I don't." She stomped his foot. Her bare feet were no match for the biker's boots. She shoved her elbow in his ribs. It didn't faze him.

Sirens blared in the distance. Dagger looked beyond Justin.

"It's over, Dagger. You can't get away." Justin took another step toward him.

The biker gripped her around the waist, lifting her off the ground and ran. Justin bolted after him.

He had to get a clear shot. She swung her fists wildly. She slipped from his grip and before Dagger could get another hold on her, Justin fired. The biker arched his back and dropped her.

She ran to him and threw herself into his arms.

"Are you all right?" He held her with one hand. Dagger wasn't moving.

She nodded.

Together they walked to the downed man. Justin knelt beside him and pressed his fingers to Dagger's neck. He got a weak pulse. "Hold on, we'll get help."

Dagger grabbed his arm. "I ain't going to jail." He coughed up blood. "Tell Mara it's in the tattoo." He released his grip, choked, and closed his eyes.

In the house, Justin explained to the police what he knew, Mara filled in the rest. The ambulance took Mrs. Butler to the hospital. Mara rode with her.

He followed in the car. After learning the older woman had a nasty bump and had fainted, the doctor assured them she would be fine and could go home, they drove back to the house.

While Mara sat with her grandmother, he stepped outside and called Rex.

"Did he say anything before he died?" Rex asked.

"As a matter of fact he did. It didn't make sense. He said to tell Mara it's in the tattoo. She only has one tiny one on her hip. She said Ran had insisted it was Greek for his devotion to her."

"Take a close-up with your phone and send it to me. Agent Patterson called this morning. I didn't want to call while you're on your honeymoon. Dixie was found murdered. Dagger's prints were all over the room." Rex informed him.

"Oh, God. She'll be devastated."

The brothers ended their conversation and Justin entered the house and met her walking into the kitchen.

"Grandmother is sleeping."

He hugged her. "That was too close." He eased her over to a chair. "I spoke to Rex. He contacted the FBI in Houston and they let the police know Dagger was on their list of most wanted so I didn't have to go down town to give a statement. The biker they picked up in New Mexico had Daggers driver's license and looked a lot like him. That's why they thought he had been caught."

"Good. I'm glad it's over." Her hands were shaking as she poured a glass of tea.

"There's something else."

She looked up. "They found Dixie murdered this morning."

Mara gasped and dropped the glass. It broke and tea splattered everywhere. "No. Oh, God, no." She hung her head.

He wrapped his arms around her. "Rex said Dagger's prints were all over the room. I'm so sorry, baby."

He let her absorb the fact that her friend had been killed. Once she calmed, he led her to their room. He held her while she slept. She had been through so much.

The next morning he called The Pink Titty in Las Vegas and spoke to the owner. "Is there going to be a service for Dixie?"

"She was cremated. She had no known relatives. We're holding a little memorial for her here but nothing fancy." The owner told him.

"I'll tell Mara. She might want to come, I'll ask. Thanks." Justin started to hang up and the owner stopped him.

"What do you want me to do with Mara's Harley?"

He had forgotten about the bike. "I'll have it shipped to Texas. I'm sure she'll want it."

He told her what Dagger had said about the tattoo. She agreed to let him take a picture and send it to Rex. A couple of days later Rex called.

"Those Greek letters are actually numbers to the bank account in the Caymans. There are millions in it. The government has taken control of the account," Rex informed him.

After he spoke to Rex, Justin called Mara into the study. He took her hand. "Rex called. The tattoo is symbols that represent numbers to an overseas bank account."

Her hand flew to her neck. "I want it removed. As soon as we get home."

He assured her they would take care of it.

***

Mara insisted that Mrs. Butler take it easy for the next few days. The older woman resisted. She finally relinquished with a promise from the couple they wouldn't leave.

He told her about the memorial for Dixie. She didn't want to go back to Las Vegas.

"She's not there. Only her ashes. I can't help her now. But I will always carry a part of her in my heart." She sobbed.

They spent the next five days making sure Mrs. Butler recovered. Hours of discussions and tales of her mother's childhood kept both women busy. She asked questions, Mrs. Butler answered. The house was Mara's sanctuary. No one wanted to leave even though Mrs. Butler offered dinner out and sight-seeing tours.

"Mrs. Butler—"

The older woman placed her hand on Mara's arm. "Please. You are my granddaughter and I want you to call me Grandmother."

She smiled at her. "Grandmother. I love the sound of that. When did you stop looking for my mother?"

The old woman's grayish blue eyes clouded over. "I stopped searching for her when they contacted me and advised me of her death. The state of Nevada found my name and address in some papers Jessica had. We had her body flown here and buried in our family plot. She is next to Gerald now. That's when I found out she had a child. I started searching for you. By then you were long gone into the foster system. Social services didn't even know where you were most of the time. My private investigator would track a home where you were supposed to be living and find you'd been moved or later, run away. Not that I blamed you after he told me the living conditions in most of the places. If only I had found you sooner!"

She wrapped her arms around the woman. "I'm so glad Justin found you. There has been a major void in my life for a long time. I always wondered if there was anyone out there who missed me."

"There is something else I need to show you." Her grandmother rose and walked over to a large painting of the house with all the flowers in full bloom. She pulled on the side and the painting swung open, revealing a wall safe.

"Is that an original Thomas Kinkade?" Justin moved closer and examined the painting.

"You know your artist. Thomas was a close friend of Gerald's. They spent a lot of time in Alaska, salmon fishing. It was a great loss when he died. Thomas did this painting for our twenty-fifth anniversary." She continued the task of opening the safe. Once the door opened, she removed a thick folder and brought it to the desk. "Come closer, Mara. You too, Justin."

Mrs. Butler sorted through a mound of papers. When she had them in the order she wanted she revealed a shocker to Mara. "The day Jessica was born Gerald set up a trust fund for her. He continued to deposit into that account until we learned of her death. We then transferred the money to another trust account where we were the signatories. After Gerald's death I made the payments. I would have stopped if I hadn't learned about you. So I continued in hopes of one day putting my granddaughter's name on it. The money now belongs to you, Mara. For you to do with whatever you want." She slid papers across the desk. Justin glanced over her shoulder and gasped.

Mara looked up at him. "What do you see?"

"If I'm looking at it correctly there are millions in the account."

She looked at her grandmother. "I can't take this money. It belonged to my mother."

The older woman smiled, amused. "But she's gone and there isn't anyone else it can go to but charity. That's where it would go if I hadn't found you. It's yours now. We'll go to the attorney's today and get it transferred over into your name."

The news both stunned her and excited her at the same time. She had no idea her mother had come from money. Only a few years earlier she had slept in flop houses, stolen for food and dug in garbage cans outside of restaurants for scraps.

"I know exactly what I want to do with it. We'll be partners in the animal clinic. You won't have to borrow money for medical equipment and we can make it bigger."

He kissed her cheek. "We'll go to an investment firm and put it in an account so you can get to it any time. I don't want you to make any decisions until you've had time to think about it."

"Thank you, grandmother. I don't know how to thank you properly. Not for the money but for never giving up on finding me. For being a kind, generous woman, for loving me. My sisters-in-law--I guess mine, too now--are planning a reception for us when we return to the ranch. It would make me so happy if you would come. I'll have my family there."

"I would love to come. Just let me know when and I'll get William to drive me."

"We're going to be leaving this afternoon and you promised to show me my mother's room. Is that something that we can do before we go to the attorney's?"

"Of course. I had almost forgot. I used to go in that room every day. Let's do that now."

Mara held Justin's hand and they followed her grandmother upstairs. The older woman turned right at the top of the stairs and stopped about half way down the hall. She removed a key from her pocket, inserted it, and the door swung open to a bright pink and purple room. The walls were covered in rock star posters from the eighties. "It's exactly the way she left it. The housekeeper comes in to dust but I won't let anyone else in here."

Mara strolled around the room, touching the mementos, opening drawers at random until she found her mother's diary. She sat on the bed and forced the book open. The door closed. She was alone with the memories of her mother. She curled up on the black and white comforter and dove into the teen years of a woman she knew very little about.

Two hours later she walked into the living room. Justin rose and she looked at him through her tears. She wiped her eyes and held out the diary to her grandmother.

"Her thoughts and fears are the same as mine have been for years."

"I couldn't bring myself to read it. I was afraid it would say how much she hated me and wanted to leave. We fought a lot before she disappeared." Tears clouded her grandmother's eyes.

Mara sat beside her. "She admired you. She never said it, but the words were there, she loved you both dearly."

Mrs. Butler burst into tears and covered her face. "I didn't know. We fought all the time. The arguments didn't amount to much but they always left me drained. I never felt they were resolved. At first it was normal teenager stuff. Then she turned bitter and self-contained after she met your father." She wiped her eyes.

***

William knocked lightly and advised lunch was ready. They followed him into the dining room and enjoyed a light lunch.

Justin eased his chair back and held Mrs. Butler's chair and took Mara's hand. They followed the older woman into the living room.

Mara took a seat. "When do we need to get back?" She asked Justin.

"I was going to tell you later that I received a call from the architect this morning. He needs me to make some decisions on the clinic. I need to get back to Tyler. You can stay as long as you like. I'll come back for you when you're ready," he informed her.

"I would love to stay, but I want to go home with you. Now that I know where Grandmother is, I can come back whenever I want." She smiled at him.

"We still have to go to the attorney's," her grandmother said.

He kissed her cheek. "We'll leave this afternoon after you and Mrs. Butler finish your business."

A short time later Mara left for the investment firm with her grandmother. He stayed behind and gathered their things. He carried the bags downstairs and put them in the car. He would miss the older woman. He knew his mother would love her and couldn't wait for them to meet.

He had their clothes packed and decided to check out the grounds in the daytime. The pool where he had chased after Dagger was an in-ground Olympic size. A pool house sat at one end. A comfortable chair provided the warmth of the sun and a clear view of the hummingbirds enjoying the feeders. Memories of the other night flooded his thoughts. He thanked God that it hadn't turned out worse than it did.

An hour later he heard the car pull in the drive and he rose. The women had done a little shopping if all the packages they hauled out of the Cadillac were any indication. He helped carry their purchases inside. Why women bought things and then had to go through and look at everything was beyond him. He dutifully sat with them and gave his approval when they asked.

With Mara's new clothes and shoes packed in a borrowed suit case and loaded into the car, they were ready to leave.

She held onto her newfound grandmother like it was the last time she would see her. "I'll be back. I promise. Every chance I get. And I want you to come to the ranch. You will love it."

With tears in her eyes, Mrs. Butler agreed. Mara waved until she could no longer see the house.

"We'll be home in three and a half hours. You okay with that?"

"I've never been happier, and it's because I attacked you at the casino and forced you to come with me. I bet you didn't think you would be doing a lot of gambling on a normal convention."

"How do you figure that?"

"You gambled on going with me that night; trusted me to help you in the desert; you stood up to your brothers to build the clinic; married me when you only knew me a couple of weeks; and took it upon yourself to find my only living family without asking me first."

"If I had asked would you have agreed?"

"Probably not. I was too scared of what I'd find."

"And now?"

She scooted over as far as the seatbelt would allow and lay her head on his shoulder. "Now. I've found my soulmate, the only man I'll ever love, and I'm about to embark on a new adventure of trying out school and becoming a vet's assistant. I'm so happy, I could cry."

"I love you Mara and I want to spend my life with you. Can we have a dozen kids?"

"Maybe three kids and a dozen dogs."

"Sounds like a plan." He kissed the top of her head.

The End

About the Author

Carol Braswell lives in East Texas with her hero husband and three spoiled Maltese. She has been creating stories since she was in the fourth grade. She took writing seriously eight years ago and wrote her first novel. After working eighteen years for the State of Texas, she quit her job to pursue two of her passions. Traveling with her husband and writing. Her first book was picked up by a publishing company and released eight years ago. After hearing another successful author speak, Mrs. Braswell decided that indie publishing was the way to go. She wrote a three book series and published them herself. A lot of action, sexy romance and personal change for the characters is in every book. She loves reading suspenseful stories with hot romance thrown in to keep things exciting.

She is a big advocate against animal abuse and supports her local no kill shelter. Her current work in progress is about murder, kidnapping, a girl with temporary amnesia, and a small town sheriff. Action packed novels are her favorite to read and write.

A sheriff who hasn't arrested anyone since JC was found in the front seat of his truck with his pants pulled down around his ankles trying to see what bit him on his ding-dong. Awkward.

You can follow Carol at:

Website: www.carolbraswell.com

Twitter: https://twitter.com/AuthorCarolB

Facebook:https://www.facebook.com/#!/carolbraswellauthor